INTO the VELVET

DARKNESS

I0550415

An Eclectic Collection of Shorts

BY

KAT YARES

Other books by Kat Yares

Beneath The Tor
The XIII
Vengeance is Mine

© 2014 by Kat Yares
ISBN 13: 978-0692311141

For Kevin:
My Husband, Soulmate, Best Friend and staunchest supporter. Thank you for always believing in me and accepting me just the way I am.

Contents

A CHILD IS BORN

A child is born. No different from millions of children born before or after. Just another birth to proud and happy parents, who look upon him as their pride and joy. Like all parents, nothing but the best hopes and dreams for their infant son.

They don't notice the intense way this baby makes its demands. They pass off irritability in the early months as colic. They ignore the fact that this child doesn't like to cuddle and has seemingly no need for touching or playful interaction.

The child reaches toddler-hood and is willful and determined. Temper tantrums are frequent, but are seen as nothing more than the terrible two's. The parents' patiently wait this stage out.

As he advances to four and five, sometimes there are still outbursts. He seems spoiled and stubborn. The child screams at his parents' hateful, hurtful things such as "I hate you! I can't wait to grow up and leave you!" The bewildered parents hope that it is just another phase and that this too shall pass.

By the time the child has aged to seven or eight, he has become smarter. He knows now that the best way to manipulate others is to appear to be what they want. Becoming the perfect child, he does his chores willingly, his homework diligently. He is the perfect little gentleman in public and though he has no friends, his parents and teachers do not worry much. After all, he has always been a loner.

Once he has matured to his teen-age years, he is every parent's dream. He is nothing like other kids his age with rock and roll on the stereo and his hair done in the latest fad style. No, this kid is impressive. His appearance is neat, but not nerdy. He is polite and helpful to all those around him. He pulls straight A's in his schoolwork and is talking about attending Harvard. He even goes to church on Sunday. This child is on his way to the top.

After high-school graduation, he goes on to his Ivy League College. Like a dutiful son, he spends vacations and breaks at home. He spends time with his family and his high school sweetheart. He still enjoys his time alone and often will take his car for a late evening drive.

The parents have yet to connect the stories of murder in the morning papers with their son. They haven't yet added one plus one and realized the deaths only happen when he is at home.

Returning home, the college graduate marries his long time girl. Settling down into a comfortable job and family life, he seems destined to become one of the town's most upstanding citizens. His loving wife understands his need for privacy, so never questions the few hours' every couple of weeks or so that he spends alone, away from her. The murders continue.

As the years pass, the killings become more frequent. He has to kill, to release the rage and resentment that has festered within him all his life. Without that outlet, he would break and not be able to keep up his appearances of normalcy.

His reputation is solid in town; he never considers that he will be caught. After all, why should anyone suspect him? He becomes so sure of himself;

he gets careless and makes mistakes. Eventually, he is arrested and convicted of murder.

His parents and wife are in a state of shock. They look back over their lives together and try to determine what they did wrong. What happened to their golden boy? Why did he turn out this way?

His mother will take it the hardest. She will lie in her bed at night and search her memory for rhyme or reason to the whole situation. Though she has been the best mother possible, always being there for him and making many sacrifices to be sure he had all he wanted, the guilt will quickly make an old woman out of a lady that had once seemed younger than her years.

His father will go to his grave believing in his son's innocence. He is convinced that someone, jealous of his child's status in life, has framed him for the many murders that have occurred. His boy is not capable of the atrocious crimes that he has been found guilty of.

His wife will take their children and quietly leave town. She cannot bear the shame. She thanks God that the children are young enough to forget their father. Maybe in a new place, where no one knows the truth, she will too.

Of course, no one remembers the tiny housefly that landed on his face the first day they brought him home. Worse even, they could not see the microscopic organism that went from the wing of the fly into his ear canal, invading his brain, before they could brush the insect away from the infant.

Moreover, they cannot know that when he hung himself in his cell, that same organism attached itself to another fly and went in search of the next perfect child that was born.

A MATTER OF WILL

He saw her immediately for what she was: a killer of his kind. Yet, in every man's existence, he must come face to face with the only circumstance that can bring him death.

He had been warned, early in life by his mentor, about women like her. Few like her existed, less than men like him. Alexander Coffey, Alex, had told him over and over in his youth that one was too many.

Cal Harper searched the room for a vantage-point. Somewhere he could keep his eyes on the woman and, escape most of the noise to think. Slowly, he surveyed the room, aware that she was watching him. Allowing his eyes to follow the staircase, he saw a loft above that would serve his needs.

Half-hoping and half-afraid that she would follow, he made his way across the floor and up the stairs. Reaching the top, he saw a stool in the far corner. Taking a seat, he could watch the party going on below him.

He thought about Alex and how he had led him into this life. Of how many years it had been since he had last seen him. Of how he missed his guidance and tutelage. Of how badly he needed his advice now.

Cal was drawn to this woman by a force unseen. They both knew exactly what the other was. He had spent his life trying to avoid a woman such as she; as she had spent hers searching for men like him.

He watched as she mingled with the crowd below. Now and again she would stop, apparently in mid-sentence, and look toward where he sat. He saw her beauty first, and a sense of awe overtook him. Her long dark hair had the color and sheen of polished Hematite, catching the rays of the soft lighting. Her eyes were green as Chinese Jade and held a coldness that reminded him of that same stone. Her skin was flawless, the make-up perfect. Her lips were red and wet, as if she had just applied a cherry gloss, though he knew she wore none. Her body, dressed in absolute black, was a statement of perfection. Cal knew he should flee, leave town, anything to get away. Yet at the same time, he knew he had to stay and meet the challenge she presented. To himself, he asked, "Oh, Alex, where are you when I need you most?"

Cal watched as she made her way to the staircase, stopping here and there for a moment of conversation. Closing his eyes, he tried to evoke the power of the ages to protect him. He knew his will was strong, but the knowledge was there that hers might be stronger. Before this night was over, one of them would cease to be. It was all a matter of whose power was the greatest.

Her voice brought him back to the moment, asking, "Don't you think it's time we met, my friend?" The voice was icy, with each word carefully formed.

"I suppose it was unavoidable, wasn't it?" Cal answered.

"Shall we take a walk on the grounds, Calvin? After all, we should get to know one another better, should we not?"

Knowing it was too late to run; Cal followed her down the stairs. Allowing her to lead the way, they went through the kitchen and out the rear door. Outside, he looked at the night. The moon was full, misted with a hazy ring. Stars twinkled and the air was still. Until now, the night had always been his friend, his ally, but tonight he sensed it could be his doom.

"You should have left when you had the chance, Calvin. I've beaten better men than you."

If he had been a normal man, her words would have sent chills down his spine. As it was, he knew he had to garner all of his strength to have a fighting chance against her.

"Am I permitted to know your name? It only seems fair, as you seem to know mine." Cal asked, trying to postpone the inevitable.

"I am known by the name of Lucy Helsing. Of course, that is not my given name. But I feel it is much more appropriate, don't you agree?"

Cal thought to himself that it indeed suited her. He knew that it had been chosen straight from the pages of Bram Stokers famous book. It was indeed a perfect name for a woman such as her.

As they walked and talked, he once more took note of her graceful beauty. He knew that no mere mortal man would be able to resist her charms, as he himself, was no mere mortal. Cal had spent centuries walking the earth by night and had never denied himself, his pleasures. It would definitely be a pleasure to take this woman, Lucy Helsing. He would only have to keep his concentration steady, then his will would be strong enough to overpower hers. Cal knew that her defeat was possible.

He thought again of Alex and his words, "You must take extreme care with one of her kind. You can not, absolutely forbid yourself, to enjoy the moment of the taking. Your only thought must be the destruction of your enemy. Do not let her beauty beguile you, lead you astray. Never let your guard down, not even for a moment, or you will be lost."

"But how will I know her?" Cal had asked.

"You will know her the instant you see her. You will be drawn to her, like no other woman before. You will be unable to resist, unable to walk away, unable to do anything except meet the challenge before you. The only advice I can give you, if you think she has found you, is to quickly move on. As far as you can possibly go."

Alex ended the discussion the same way he always had on the subject, "My son, don't tempt the fates that be. Avoid her kind as you would the bright sunshine."

Now Cal found himself in the situation where it was impossible to flee. They were here, together, and only one would leave this night alive. He could only hope he was strong enough.

They, Cal and Lucy, came to a stop under an ancient elm tree. The moonlight was filtering through the tree's branches. Cal thought to himself that this would be a perfect place for a taking, if only circumstances were different.

He turned to face Lucy, finding that she had already shed her jacket and was undoing the buttons on her blouse. Allowing it to fall from her shoulders, she gazed at him steadily and said simply, "Shall we begin?"

Placing his hands on her shoulders, he pulled her closer, never taking his eyes from hers. Feeling her body molded next to his, he knew her blood would taste exquisite. He thought of how her strength, mingled with his, would increase his power. Caressing her face with his lips, he followed the contours of her bones to her neck. Momentarily drawing back, he bared his fangs, then buried them in the soft skin of her throat.

As he drank he felt, what he was sure was what the human male felt when he reached orgasm. Unable to control the sensations and feelings, he knew in his dark heart that he had lost. Momentarily, he felt his life force being drawn from him. "But wait!" he thought, "Had he just felt her talons, that were once graceful fingers, buried in his back, ease their grip?" Putting as much of his concentration as possible on the taking, he knew the longer he could hold out the more hope he had. Yes, the talons were loosening, he was sure of that now.

No longer was he losing. He could feel his energy growing. Moments later, he felt not only her nails recede but also her entire body slacken against him. Knowing his victory was near; he drank greedily, sucking the blood and life from her limp body.

When nothing was left, he released her and watched as she fell to the ground. Picking up her jacket, he wiped the blood from his mouth. Her body was aging fast, as his would, had she won. Minutes later, she had returned to dust. As he picked up her clothing, Cal thought he had never felt so good in his entire existence. Walking to his car, he felt his spirits soar. Now he had a reason to party. After stashing her clothing under the spare tire of his black Jaguar, he turned and headed back to the house.

On his way up the walk, a voice sounded in the darkness, "You have done well, my son."

Cal laughed as Alex emerged from the night.

ANY WHERE BUT HERE

I heard the craziest story the other day. First, let me back up to the beginning. I was driving down the interstate, doing somewhere between seventy-five and eighty, and I saw this guy hitching. He was holding a sign that said simply 'ANY WHERE BUT HERE'. Being a curious sort, I flashed my lights and pulled over.

Running the hundred or so yards to my car, he jumped in on the passenger side.

"Thank God you stopped, Mister. I've been out there all day." He said, friendly enough, but I noticed he didn't smile.

"About to give up, huh?" I answered back, trying to be cordial. "What's with the sign? Is it don't know or don't care where it is you're going?"

"Does it really matter which?" he asked, staring out the front window.

Glancing over at him, I replied, "Nope, I don't guess it does at that. Just curious that's all."

Neither of us said anything more for a while. The silence was broken when he asked, "How far are you going?"

"Couple hundred miles down the road," I answered, naming a small town near the state line. "I've got a sales call to make there. You going all the way with me?"

"Guess I will. By the way, I do appreciate this ride."

Falling into silence once more, I took the time to watch my passenger a little closer. The man was almost spooky to look at. He just sat there in the seat. His hands remained clenched in his lap, and he looked straight ahead out the window. We went a good fifty miles like that. I was beginning to get a bit leery of this guy. Here I was smoking like a smokestack, and although he had cigarettes in his shirt pocket, he had yet to light one.

Finally, he turned and looked at me. "Curiosity killed the cat, you know."

The way he said that sent a slight shiver through me. His words sounded more like a threat. He spoke in a flat monotone, with no hint of humor or emotion. I couldn't handle it anymore. He was making me more nervous by the minute.

"Man, what's with you? Are you running from the law? What's your story anyway?" I demanded, hearing the anger in my voice.

"If I tell you, it won't be my story any more. It will be yours. Are you sure you want to hear it?"

"Hell yes, I want to hear." I said, still with an edge in my voice.

"Just remember," he said, "once I've told you, the story becomes your story."

He paused for a short time and I noticed raindrops beginning to fall on the windshield. I turned on the wipers and looked at the sky. Briefly, I wondered where this storm had come from. It had been bright and sunny five minutes ago. I had to dismiss the thought from my mind that, somehow, my passenger was causing this storm as a prelude to his story. The lightning was ripping across the sky, appearing as giant rips in the darkness overhead. The thunder that followed was deafening, so intense that it shook the car.

Glancing over at him, I almost yelled, "Well, get on with it, I'm waiting."

He looked at me, and for a moment, a half smile formed on his lips.

"Tell me, do you believe in fairies?" he asked, no longer smiling.

"Fairies as in queers or as in Peter Pan?" I answered trying to suppress a grin.

"Fairies as in old folk tales, especially the ones from Ireland. You are Irish, aren't you?" he asked.

"Yes, I'm Irish. What has that got to do with anything? Those old folk tales are just myths, the kind of stories a mother tells her kids to get them to behave." I countered, thinking I had a real loony in the car. He must have escaped from a mental hospital or something. Deciding to humor him a bit, I added, "I suppose most myths have some truth behind them, right?"

"I'll let you decide that for yourself," he said, "after I finish my story."

"Fair enough" I replied. The thought crossed my mind that I should stop the car and put him out. But, what if he had a weapon? I decided to just keep driving and bide my time until I could figure how to get rid of him safely.

He began his story.

"Way back in time, where legends and myths began, there was an evil breed of fairies called the Redcaps. These were the most malevolent creatures in the entire fairy realm. They used to live in old ruined towers and castles, the kind of places that had a history of wickedness. As time passed, places such as that disappeared. Therefore, they had to evolve. Over the generations, they mutated to where now they search out and trade places with a human. This person has to have two special qualifications. First he has to be of full Irish blood and second he has to have malice and resentment against mankind in his heart."

Turning toward him, I said, "That sounds more like my wife."

"They cannot inhabit a female, there are other fairies for them. Let me continue; now you know a little history of the Redcaps. So I'll tell you how I came to meet one."

Looking over at him, I realized that this man was completely insane. Then I noticed the red hat on his head and shivered.

"I'm not real sure I want to hear anymore. I mean, it's a pleasant story and all, but do you really expect me to believe it?" I asked, attempting to hide a chuckle. I believed at this point the guy was just nuts, not dangerous.

"You said you wanted to hear this," he said, stomping his feet against the floor board, "let me finish."

"All right, all right, go ahead. Sorry I interrupted." I said.

"You know, once I used to be like you. A salesman, I used to sell prefabricated metal products. Then one day, I met with a client. He was quiet and moody. We went to lunch and it was like pulling teeth to get him to talk. Well, after a while, I got upset and just like you, I demanded he tell me his story. He told me the same fable I've told you. He went on to tell me that he was a Redcap, and had been for more than a year. His body was wearing out and it was time to find a replacement. He told me about the murders and the evil he had done. First, he killed his wife, then his boss and on and on till he had destroyed everyone he cared about. Once they were dead, he would drop his cap in their blood. By the way, that's how they got their name, Redcaps, because they dyed their hats in their victims' blood. Anyhow, I was like you, I didn't believe him. I thought the man was off in the head. However, after lunch, as we walked back to our cars, he died and I became a Redcap. And now, here we sit."

Before I could comment, the back tire blew.

"Damn, now I've got to change the frigging tire. In this rain too. Maybe you think you're a fairy of some kind, but the least you can do, is come help get this over." I said, thinking to myself that once we had the tire changed, I'd take off fast, leaving him behind.

We got out of the car and walked around to the trunk. Opening it and pulling out the spare, he reached in to get the tire iron. I immediately put out my hand to take it from him. The moment I grabbed the other end, lightning struck and I could feel the current rushing through my body.

With-in seconds, the man fell to the ground. Looking up at me, he said, "Finally it's over."

The rain stopped as suddenly as it had appeared. Up the road I could see the sign for a gas station. Cursing the circumstances, I started sprinting up the road, hoping to find a telephone. Reaching the station, I had the attendant call the local sheriff.

Several hours later, I was back on the road. This hitchhiker's death was attributed to a freak act of nature. I went on to my sales meeting and thought no more about my strange passenger. The next day, I returned home and told my wife and children about the strange story he had told me. They agreed that the man had to be crazy to come up with something like that.

Later, on the evening news, I learned that the man was wanted for killing his entire family. His wife, parents' and sister had all died by his hand. Several other murders around the country were credited to him. I had the feeling that I had been very lucky.

This all happened about a week ago. Today I'm back on the road. Everything is different now. I have a red hat on my head. I don't know where I'm going. Just any where but here.

BED ROCKS

It was the old man's last day on the job. A logger by trade, this would be the final time he would have to be in the woods for pay. He was glad it was over, he had come to hate every minute he has to spend outdoors cutting down trees to give the rich folks their fine wood furniture.

Four hours to go and he would be able to leave the woods forever. The rest of the day he planned to just sluff off. He was tired and looked around for a place to sit. After wandering around a bit, he found a large oak tree marked with the big blue "X" denoting that it wasn't to be cut. Sitting down at the base of the trunk, he adjusted his ball cap to shade the sun from his eyes.

Looking out at the ravaged landscape his eyes caught sight of two rounded rocks lying side by side. The conversation from the morning echoed in his head.

"Henry, you've got to find us new bed rocks while you're out in the woods today."

"I will." He had replied, half listening to his wife of forty-five years.

"I don't want to have to climb into cold sheets again. Do you hear me, Henry."

"I hear you, Martha. I hear you."

Deciding that it was best to check the rocks out before he got too comfortable, he lazily got to his feet. Although his wife could be a nag, he did still love her just as much as when they were first dating almost a half a century ago. He had to admit that he liked slipping into a warm bed himself. Their last set of bed rocks had split last spring from twenty years of repeated warming on the wood stove. If these two rocks were suitable, he knew that he would probably never have to replace them, as he would be dead before they broke also.

Slowly he bent over and picked up one of the rocks. About the size of a round loaf of pumpernickel, he could feel the heft of the rock. Taking his glasses from his shirt pocket and putting them on, he examined the rock for cracks. There did not appear to be any, yet the entire surface was covered with tiny fossilized shells. He sat it back on the ground and picked up the second one. Almost a twin of the first, not just in size and weight, but also covered with the tiny fossils.

"Martha will like these." He said to himself.

They were almost pretty and she probably wouldn't hide them away in a closet when spring came around again. He picked up the first rock and carried them both back to the tree where he was sitting before. It did not take long before the old man was dozing, waiting to hear the truck horn blow, signaling quitting time. Later he gave the rocks to his wife, who after first glance unceremoniously dumped them into the sudsy dish water.

"They'll probably be real pretty once they're cleaned up. Thank you, Henry."

Taking the potato scrubber, she began to wash the rocks. Once she was satisfied with their cleanliness, she took them one at a time and sat them on the wood stove to dry and warm.

That night, thirty minutes before bed as was her habit, she removed the rocks and wrapped them in heavy terry cloth towels. Placing them between the sheets in the middle part of the bed, she anticipated the warmness of the bed.

Other than the back and forth from bed to woodstove and back, nothing more was said about the bedrocks. They were all but forgotten in the daily routine.

A week later, Henry got up from bed and began rubbing his back. Going into the kitchen, he found Martha making breakfast.

"Did you turn the mattress, Martha?"

"No, I won't be doing that until spring. Why?"

"I don't know," he replied, "the bed just seemed harder last night, that's all."

"I didn't notice any difference."

"Well, maybe it was just the way I slept."

Later that day, Martha went in and stripped the bed to wash the bed sheets. Sitting down on Henry's side of the bed, she could feel no real difference. She dismissed her husband's complaints from her mind. Another week passed, before the subject of the bed was brought up again.

"I just don't know Martha, but I swear the bed is getting harder." Henry felt like his back had a thousand bruises on it. It ached for him to walk across the floor.

"Well, I suppose we could go ahead and turn the mattress. That should take care of the problem. If not, I guess we need to buy a new one."

She knew that would shut him up for a while anyway. Henry hated to spend money, especially on anything for the house, no matter how comfortable it would make him.

He raised an eyebrow at his wife.

"Well, let me know when you're ready and I'll help you."

"That's ok, I can do it. Besides I don't want to hear any more of your whining about your back today."

As Martha turned the mattress, she did notice that it was getting lumpier in some places. One spot, down toward where Henry's feet should have been actually made a crunching noise as the bedding caught on the corner bending. When the mattress was in position on the box springs, Martha sat down on the bed.

"Much better." She thought and gave it a little bounce. No sound now and there didn't seem to be any lumps.

"Must have been my imagination," she said aloud, then laughed, "Isn't any wonder, what with all the grumbling Henry's been doing."

Nothing more was said about the bed, other than Henry stating the next morning that it was much better and that the turning must have done the trick.

Several weeks later, they left for a weekend trip to see their son in Atlanta. John was their pride and joy, an only child; he had excelled in everything he had ever attempted. Now he was a microbiologist for the government. Henry had made many sacrifices for his son's education and had never regretted a one of them. Anything to keep his son from following in his footsteps working as a logger.

John had always been enthralled with bugs, especially the ones you could only see under a microscope. When he had been younger, mites had been his supreme attraction. For sure, chicken and dander mites had been plentiful around his home growing up. Now with his job at the Center of Disease Control, he had the opportunity to get paid for his fascinations with the microscopic creatures.

Martha and Henry had been looking forward to this trip since Henry planned his retirement back in the spring. John and promised them dinner out and possibly the theatre, depending upon what play was in town. Martha had bought a new dress and Henry had packed his one suit for the occasion.

The weekend went well and when Sunday morning rolled around, they had been wined and dined and otherwise treated as royalty by their son. Putting the two suitcases into the rear of the battered Suburban, Henry couldn't help but wonder when they would be able to afford another trip like this. Martha adored her son, but now with no income other than his social security to live on, he knew these trips would be less frequent. John never seemed to have time to come home except at Christmas and occasionally on his mother's birthday.

Henry pulled the car out into traffic and began the ten-hour journey home. He figured to be there by midnight, but due to a wreck on the interstate he was off by several hours. It took another thirty minutes to get a fire going strong in the wood stove. Almost as an afterthought he turned to Martha.

"Have you called John yet?"

"Henry, it's three in the morning."

"I know, but we did promise to call when we got here. I'd hate to think he might be waiting up."

"Well, you call him then." She replied.

She walked over to the stove and touched the bedrocks.

"Warm enough." She declared and reached for the towels hanging on the hook beside the stove.

"I'm going to bed. Try to make it quick, all right Henry?"

"I will. Be there in a minute."

Henry walked to the kitchen and dialed the phone.

"Morning Son, sorry if I woke you, but we just got in."

"That's all right Dad. I'm glad to know you made it. Any problems?"

"No, just a tractor trailer overturned on the interstate and kept traffic backed up. I'll tell you all about it next time we talk, right now, I'm going to join your mother in the bed. I'm beat."

"OK, Dad. Go get some rest. I'll call you Sunday at the regular time."

"Talk to you then son." Henry said and then hung up the phone.

Sunday came and the phone in the kitchen began to ring. No one answered.

Two cars pulled into the driveway on Wednesday morning. One was the sheriff; the other was John who had become concerned when the phone had gone unanswered for the past two days.

"That's your dad's car isn't it, John?" The sheriff asked as he joined the man in the drive.

"It is." He responded, searching for the correct key on his keying. Opening the door, they were first assaulted by the smell. A sour, acid odor permeated the air making them both gag. The sight inside the house brought both men to a full stop.

The floors, walls, and ceiling were crawling with bugs. Large insects, unlike anything either man had seen before. For a moment, John's analytical mind took over and had the thought that they resembled the mites found in bed sheets and mattresses of every person's home. Yet he knew that was impossible, they could not be seen with the naked eye.

"Dad, Mom?" His voice barely whispered from his throat. He started to step into the living room, when he felt a hand on his shoulder.

"I can't let you go in there, John."

"I have to know."

"I know you do. But it looks like we going to need some type of protection before we go in."

"I'll call the office. Someone there can help."

As the sun reached its peak in the noonday sky, the yard was crawling not only with the bugs that had escaped from the house, but also workers from the CDC in HAZMAT uniforms. Putting on the special suits, John and the sheriff entered the house.

Stepping across the floor that now looked and felt alive, they made their way to the bedroom that John's parents had shared for over fifty years. The sheriff pulled back the covers on the bed and a muffled scream escaped from behind both men's hoods.

Nothing was left of Henry and Martha Jones except dried bones. Their skeletons still in the spooning curve of the way they had slept their entire lives together. At the foot of the bed were the bedrocks, oozing a dark gray substance into the remains of the mattress. From the mattress, hundreds more of the mite like insects scurried from inside.

MURDER BY MODEM

He sat, as he had on many previous evenings, watching the computer terminal and waited. He knew it was only a matter of time until she would sign on again. It was always that way with the lonely hearts. They were online every night, searching the new singles' bar of the nineties for Mr. Right.

Half interested, he read the lines as they scrolled off the screen. Although he had been doing this for over a year, it never ceased to amaze him, the confidences people would reveal to total strangers. He supposed they felt safe in anonymity. Yet, he knew if he handled the conversations right, the desperate ones would tell him everything about themselves. It was only a matter of gaining their trust. These women were so gullible.

* * *

The woman rushed into the small apartment, not bothering to take the time to feed the cat. She had promised Wanderer that she would sign online by eight o'clock, and it was now seven after nine. While waiting for the computer to boot up, she cursed Cheryl for not showing up at the library tonight, causing her to have to work over and be late for her 'date'. Once connected, she immediately pressed the keywords to locate him. Holding her breath, she let it go only when she found in Lobby B discussing current events with someone with the handle of NormalJoe.

Pausing, she waited for Wanderer to acknowledge her. Until she had met him, she had been too shy to participate in the conversations, but one night he had noticed her and had made a point to direct all his comments and statements to her. Since that night, three weeks ago, she had met him here every Friday night, always declining to enter a private room so as not to appear too forward or easy. Tonight, though, she figured she owed him for being late. Tonight, she would go private, if he asked.

＊ ＊ ＊

"Ah, there she is." The man said aloud, although there was no one around him to hear. For a moment or two, he decided to let her sweat, make her think he might be upset at her for being late signing on. In truth, it made no difference; he had used his time marking future contacts. By the time he finished with this one, he would have his next game already begun.

Deciding that he had allowed her to suffer long enough, he began entering words on the keyboard.

"Hello, again, BookLady. Did you have to work late tonight?"

"Sure did, Wanderer, and sometimes it makes me so upset. Especially on Friday's. I'm sure you understand why."

"Hey, no sweat. I was late signing on myself. In fact I just got here a few minutes ago."

"Oh, good, that makes me feel a little better anyway. So how was your week?"

"Same old stuff, busy as always. So what shall we talk about this evening?"

"I'm not real sure, so I'll leave that up to you." she replied.

Got her, the man thought to himself. Now he would just have to play it cool for the next hour or so. By the end of the evening, he hoped he would have not only her real name, but her address and phone number as well. Then the truly fun part would begin.

"Well then, my dear BookLady, why don't we play a game of make believe tonight?"

"What do you mean, Wan?" the woman answered.

"Let's pretend that we are about to have our first date. Something very simple. Like maybe, dinner somewhere nice. What is the best restaurant in your city?"

"The finest would have to be The Top of the Towers, its downtown and I understand it is elegant. Though I've never actually been there."

"OK, then that's where we'll meet. If it is all right with you, I'll create the room. Then I will Instant Message you and you can meet me there. I promise to behave like a perfect gentleman. You should know by now that I'm not like some people on this service. What do you say?"

"I think it might be fun." she replied, "I'll wait for your message."

A few moments later he sent the Instant Message, "Meet me in the Tower Room. I'll have the champagne ordered."

* * *

Almost giggling, Emma Spencer, began pushing the keys that would take her to the private room. She hoped she wasn't making a fool of herself, after all what did she really know about this man.

He had told her, he worked in a large hospital. She assumed he was a doctor. When she had tried to identify him online, the service just said that he was from Kansas City. They had both exchanged ballpark figures of their ages. Other than that, and the assumption that he was a gentleman, she didn't know much. Maybe she would learn more tonight.

Watching the screen change to the private room, she smiled as she saw the graphics already on the screen. Beside a picture of a mug, he had written, "Your champagne, my lady. Sorry about the mug, but for some reason, the glasses in this place are all dirty."

"That's fine, sir. A mug will do nicely."

"And, which would you prefer for our meal. . . steak, seafood or a combination of the two?"

"Oh, I don't know. Why don't you order for me, Wan?"

"Well then, let us start with Caesar salad, then have steak and lobster, and maybe finish with strawberry cheesecake? Does that sound all right?"

"That sounds perfect, Wan." was all she could reply. She wondered if this was the type of meal he treated his real dates to. If so, she felt they were very lucky.

* * *

The lines continued to flow across the screen. Between the nonsense about how she was enjoying her meal, he was asking questions about her. He tried to make the questions as casual as possible, attempting to tie them in with the questions, she, herself asked.

Before dessert was served, he had found out her full name and her private phone number. All had left to do was get her address. If he couldn't con that out of her online tonight, he had a backup plan in mind that he knew she would fall for.

Maybe for now, he thought, I should just cool my heels a bit. She had been harder to break than most of the others before her. He didn't want to go too far too fast. That might scare her off, and he felt he had invested too much of his time already to lose the chase now.

He tried to think of the easiest way to sign off for the night, finally deciding to fabricate an emergency call from the hospital. He knew that would impress her.

"BookLady, be right back, I've got to catch the other line."

He spent the next few minutes impatiently waiting for his wife to make him a cup of instant coffee. Then he turned back to the keyboard.

"Hi. I'm back. Sorry it took so long. That was the hospital on the line. It appears I'm going to have to go back in tonight. Sure hope you understand."

"Well, of course I do." She replied. "I do want to thank you for an enchanting evening though."

"That was my pleasure, I assure you. See you same time next week?" he asked.

"I wouldn't miss it." she answered. "Hope you don't have to work too hard."

"That's all part of the job. Well, until next Friday . . . take care. I've got to run."

"Goodbye Wanderer, and thanks again."

He pushed the keys to sign off the service, knowing full well that he would use another name and come back online in a few minutes. He was sure that he would find her monitoring the lobby for a while longer. Maybe he would even see if she would be friendly with what she supposed was another man. That might be interesting.

* * *

Another hour later, he turned the computer off for the night and sat back in the desk chair to study his notes. The woman's name was Emma Spencer. Fitting, he thought, a spinster image. She was thirty-five to forty years old and had worked at the library for the last seventeen years. She didn't own a car. In fact, she didn't know how to drive, relying instead on public transportation to get from one place to another. She lived alone with only a tomcat named Apple to keep her company. From the television shows she indicated she liked, he could tell she spent most evenings home alone also. She did not have any close family in town and only one close friend.

"Yes," he thought, "this one is perfect."

The sight of his wife standing on the stairway looking in the doorway at him interrupted his thoughts. She seemed undecided whether to speak or not.

"Did you want something, Maylene?" he asked.

"I was just wondering if you were coming to bed." she replied.

"Does it look like I'm ready for bed? I don't know why you continue to hound me about things. When a little common sense would give you all the answers you need." he said, rising from the chair.

He had to laugh when he heard her choked breath and the scramble of feet going up the stairs. She needed a reminder of who was boss in this house, he thought. He turned off the desk lamp and headed up the stairs, taking his belt off as he went.

* * *

Emma jerked to wakefulness. The shrill ringing of the telephone sounded alien to her ears. Barely glancing at the small digital clock, she raced from the bed toward the kitchen. Her mind registered the time, as she picked up the phone.

Saying hello into the receiver, she wondered who would be calling her at this time of night.

"Hi. Did I wake you?" the man's voice asked.

"Who is this?" she replied, sure that it was a wrong number.

"Emma, I'm sorry. I should have said straight out. This is Wanderer."

"Oh. Hello Wan. Give me a second to clear away the cobwebs. I wasn't expecting your call."

"Yes, I know. The problem is . . . I'm standing here at the airport and it hit me that today is Friday and I was going to miss our time together. So I thought I had best call and let you know why." he paused, as if waiting for a response.

"Well, I'm glad you called then. I mean, I don't know what I would have thought if you hadn't been there tonight. So where are you off to?" she asked.

"Actually, I'm heading to your state. I've got a convention to attend this weekend in Knoxville." once more he paused, waiting.

"Knoxville! Why that is where I live. I know I told you the town was Fountain City, but they incorporated years ago. To think, you're going to be right here in town." Emma's face was beginning to flush. She hoped he would ask to meet her. The idea both excited and frightened her.

"You've got to be joking?" he said, "In that case, maybe you would consider dinner tonight at The Top of the Towers?"

"I suppose that would be all right." she stopped for a moment. "Yes, I know it would be."

"Shall I pick you up around eight, then? I'll make the reservations when I get to town. Now if you will give me your address and some directions coming from downtown, we'll be all set."

* * *

As he drove down Broadway toward Fountain City, his mind began making a mental picture of what this Emma Spencer was like. For a moment or two on the phone last night, he had thought she was going to turn down his offer of dinner. This one was much surer of herself than the others had been.

Passing the small lake she had mentioned, he looked closely for the street she had named.

"Ah, there it is...Essary Road." he said, turning on his right blinker.

His anticipation was increasing. He only had about a mile and a half to go. What was it she had said? "the third house on the left after you pass Jacksonville Pike." As he slowed the car at the final four way stop, he imagined that right now she was very nervous. He knew that she had never done this type of thing before. That was why he had stopped and bought the bottle of wine. He hoped it would help break the ice before the evening got started.

Pulling into her driveway, he saw that she had left on a dim porch light for him. Other than that, the neighborhood was almost dark. A lone streetlight burned a half block away on the opposite corner.

"This is good." he said to himself as he gathered the bottle of wine and a small bouquet of silk flowers.

She opened the door moments after he rang the bell and he saw that she wasn't as plain as he had expected. In fact, a trip to the beauty parlor and a makeover at Merle Norman's would make her, if not pretty, then at least, very attractive.

In her small, galley-shaped kitchen, she was standing at the counter, still gushing her thanks for the flowers. He wondered if she would ever get around to pouring the wine he had opened for her. It had taken a bit of smooth talking, just to convince her to have a glass. She had protested that she had never drunk anything alcoholic in her life. He had reassured her that one small glass wouldn't hurt, and besides, tonight was special, wasn't it? "Well, maybe just a sip then." she reluctantly agreed.

Still chattering, she turned her back to him to reach into the cabinet for the glasses. The man stepped forward with the wine as she sat the glasses on the countertop and moved to the end of the galley. The sound of the glasses tipping over was all he heard, other than the gagging noise he made, as she tightened the phone cable around his throat.

COUNTRY PLUMBING

'If I had a dollar . . .' Myrtle Gardner thought to herself as she worked the plunger over the kitchen drain. She was, of course, thinking about her worthless son Jimmy. He had promised weeks ago to check the drain. Like the hundred promises before, he had forgotten this one also.

Myrtle could smell the vile bile rising up from the sink and knew that the leach line must be totally plugged. Giving up with the plunger, she walked the short distance to the telephone hanging on the wall. Once again she called her son.

"Jimmy, where have you been?"

"Hi Ma, what's up?"

"You're half-drunk again, ain't you Jimmy? Well that don't matter none. You get yourself over here right now and fix my sink."

"Ma, I done had a hard day at work. I ain't coming over there tonight."

"Yes, you are son. Or you can just forget me paying that truck payment for you next month."

Myrtle knew that would shake him up. Her son could barely hold down a job at all, he sure couldn't afford that fancy pickup truck he drove without her help.

"I'll be there in an hour, Ma."

"No, you'll be here in thirty minutes." Myrtle replied and hung up the phone.

Twenty-five minutes later, the young man walked through the front door.

"Now what's all the fuss about Ma?"

"The fuss, as you call it, is about the kitchen sink you promised to fix two weeks ago. Now it won't drain at all."

"Ma, if you'd just stop stuffing trash down it, I promise, it would quit clogging."

"Don't you be talking back to me. You think I don't know what stops up a sink. I haven't been putting nothing down it. Now, you just get yourself in there and get it fixed."

Jimmy shrugged and started for the kitchen.

"I hope you at least got something cooking, seeing as how you dragged me out before I could fix myself some dinner."

"I'm not going to be dirtying no dishes until I have a sink to wash them in. Reckon you're just going to have to go hungry until you get it fixed."

Cursing under his breath, Jimmy looked in the kitchen sink.

"Gee Ma, couldn't you have at least bailed the water out before I got here."

"I could have, but I didn't. If you had been here two weeks ago like you promised, you wouldn't be haven to do it now. Just fix it Jimmy and quit whining about it."

Jimmy reached over and grabbed the plunger sitting next to the cabinet. Using all his strength, he attempted to force the water down the drain.

"Tell ya what Ma, whatever it is you got down there sure is lodged tight. I'm going have to go to the truck and get my tools."

"I told ya Jimmy, it was bad."

"Sure hope it ain't in that leach line, Ma. I didn't bring my snake, just a couple of pipe wrenches."

"I don't care what you brought. I just want the thing fixed."

Jimmy headed out for his truck, "Will ya clean out the cabinet for me Ma?"

"I ain't doing none of your work for you. You can clean it out when you get back in here."

"Well, at least find me a box to put it all in."

Jimmy came back into the kitchen carrying two wrenches. He was surprised to find that his mother had brought a large milk carton box to hold the many cleaning supplies she stored under the sink. Opening the cabinet, he began filling the box.

"I'm going to need another box, Ma." He said, when the first was full.

"I ain't got no more." Came the reply, "You're just going to have to make do."

After stacking everything on top of each other in the box, Jimmy finally got the large space emptied. How anybody could fill the equivalent of three kitchen cabinets with half-empty bottles of cleaning supplies was beyond him. He could bet he had no more than a bottle of bleach and a few rags under his kitchen sink.

"You still dating that white trash that lives up the road?"

"Ma, she ain't white trash. You just don't like her because she keeps those snakes."

"Well, any woman that likes snakes has to be off in the head, or just pure trash or something. No decent woman would."

Not being able to resist the temptation, Jimmy said,

"Well you know Ma, one of her pythons got loose back in the spring. Ain't never found it."

Jimmy had a smile on his face, which should shut her up for a minute or two. Turning off the water to the faucet, he placed a bucket under the pipe, took the pipe wrenches, and began undoing the "S" shaped drainpipe. After the sink water had drained into the bucket, he unscrewed the bottom of the pipe. Pulling out the "S" pipe, he looked at it and saw that it was clean.

"Damnit, Ma, you must have something clogged in the line leading to the leach."

He only hoped that was what it was, he was in no way prepared to clean out the leach line tonight and could just imagine the tongue lashing he would get if his mother did not have running water before it got full dark.

Rolling to his belly, he used the wrenches to unhook the pipe leading to the leach line. Why anyone would have a one and three quarter pipe going into a four-inch line was beyond him.

"Jimmy, you did cover up that hole where the rats got into the leach during the summer, didn't ya?"

"Sure I did, Ma." He replied, knowing full well that he didn't. That little chore had been forgotten, the minute he had cleaned out the rat's nest at the end of the leach line earlier in the year.

The connection was giving him fits; it did not want to come loose. Positioning himself closer to the pipe, he finally felt it give way. His mother was still prattling outside the cabinet, but he had shut her out. One final twist and the fitting came loose and he pulled it away. Immediately he saw what had clogged the drain, but it was too late to move. His head was enveloped.

Myrtle stood, leaning against the cabinet berating her son for his shortcomings when she saw his feet kicking against the carpet. She yelled at him to quit fooling around. Getting no answer, she looked under the cabinet, only to see her son's body totally devoured up to the shoulders by the python that was still streaming out of the leach line. All Myrtle could do was scream, as the snake continued to slither out of the pipe filling the entire space of the cabinet.

THE CRYSTAL

The woman sat and stared into the facets of the crystal. Into its depths, she searched for the visions that she had come to expect. She had received this particular quartz crystal several months ago as a gift. At the time she had thought it nothing more than a pretty rock. The amazing powers, the stone was said to possess, were to her, just a folk tale.

The first night she sat and held it, she was surprised to feel warmth generating from its base. Her curiosity was aroused. She began holding it whenever she had a free minute. Each time, she felt more of its influence. She found that she was becoming obsessed with it. She carried it everywhere she went, tucked into her pocket or her bra, to keep the energy close to her. She slept with the stone in her left hand at night to receive its messages in her dreams. She discovered that she could no longer make even the simplest of decisions without meditating with the stone.

Her personal and professional life began to suffer. As the days passed, nothing else mattered except the stone. She no longer dated. She had called in sick to work so many times in the last two weeks that this morning, she had been fired. She didn't really care. She could no longer function without the rock in sight. Her co-workers had laughed at her when she tried to explain her fascination with the stone.

Just about a week ago was when she had seen the movement within the mists of the inner crystal. At first, the movements were barely perceptible. She had mistaken them for shadows, perhaps from the TV or tree limbs playing against the windows. The more she had gazed into the gem, the stronger and more powerful the images had become.

Well past midnight, she was finally rewarded. She had been staring at the facets for a solid two hours. Now, as she gazed, the familiar images began to appear.

First, came the form of the man. As he became clearer, she noted once again how his looks affected her. He was not handsome, in the modern sense of the word. But during his time, he must have been a striking figure. Rugged looking, dark skinned, his black hair hung straight to his shoulders in a wild, abandoned manner. His face was scarred and pock-marked and the dark, heavy mustache, made her wish she could reach out and stroke the skin and feel the scars he had earned undoubtedly in battle. His eyes were what reached deep within her, black almost ebony, with an intensity that caused her to be weak with longing for him.

The woman knew that she was somehow connected with this man. She wondered if she had been him, or his mate, sometime in a previous life. Until she had received the crystal she had not believed in reincarnation, but the bond she felt with the man had changed her mind.

She thought to herself, that since she had received the stone, her entire mind-set about many old ideas had changed. She now believed that the crystal had opened her consciousness to connect her with the cosmic mind. She knew that this was the 'enlightenment' that she and so many of her co-workers had scoffed at. She was no longer laughing. Her crystal had shown her the 'light'.

She continued to look deeply into the gem, watching as the figure of the beast formed. She had never seen anything, in any book, painting or movie, which had any remote similarity to this creature. The closest her mind could come up with was a dragon.

The monster was huge, at least five times taller than the man. Its body was massive, somewhat resembling a dinosaur, with a tail that whipped from side to side taking everything down in its path. While she had not seen it breathe fire, the animal's face and head looked like something out of a medieval painting. The horns on its head were gnarled, like pieces of old driftwood. The eyes blazed red in the green tinged face. Its mouth was large, filled with long sharp teeth and appeared frozen in a hungry grin. The wings attached to the scaly, grass colored back was what connected it in her mind to the legendary dragon of fairy tale fame.

As she watched, the beast made its way through the dense forest to where the man waited on the cliff-side. The man stood in an aggressive stance ready to do combat. She watched as the dragon entered the clearing and looked towards its adversary. The battle began.

Night after night, she had watched the struggle between man and beast. Never had she seen who had won. The images had always faded before their fates revealed themselves. Her imagination in wakefulness and dreams had been her only source of an outcome. But tonight, she sensed that it was going to be different.

The images were clearer than ever. She could make out tiny details in the surroundings that had escaped her before: the jaggedness of the rocks on the cliff-face and the shapes of the leaves on the trees. Her eyes took in the beauty of his sword, the gemstones and engraving on the hilt. She saw there what she thought to be words, yet had no idea of their meaning.

As she watched, the scene began to be frightfully real. She could feel the heat of the sun and the wind blowing against her skin. No longer were the images embedded within the crystal. They were all around her. It took her a few moments to realize that it was no longer a vision. It was now reality. She was part of it.

She looked around for a means of escape and saw none. She was standing in the clearing between the monster and the man. The cliff was at her back, the creature to her front. To either side was clear meadow that dropped off into nowhere. She struggled with panic as she realized she could only stand and watch as the battle took place.

Her mind told her this could not be happening, that she must have gone insane. Yet, she watched her knight ("Her knight? Now where did that come from?" She wondered.) stand bravely with sword and shield ready to attempt to overpower the dragon. Deep in her heart, she knew it was a vain effort. He was neither strong enough nor armed enough to win this fight.

She watched as he laid the sword aside, and stooped to pick up a crossbow. She saw the arrows fly from his bow toward the creature. She stood unbelieving as they hit its scaly armor and simply bounced off. She cringed as the talons from its forearms inflicted wound after wound on the man. Still, he would not surrender.

Exhausting his supply of arrows, he laid the crossbow aside, picked up his sword and welded it toward the dragon. The animal finally shed blood as the blade made contact and sliced through the claws of its right arm. The woman had to cover her ears to try to block the sound of the monster's screams.

In amazement, she watched as the talons began to re-grow, replacing the ones that were lost. What chance did the man have against the magic of this demon, yet he refused to give up. Valiantly he fought, although it was obvious that his strength was weakening.

Suddenly, as if not realizing it before, the woman's mind screamed at her, "If he dies, so will I". Once more seeking a means of escape, the woman took her eyes off the struggle and looked around. The monster was closer still to her and she could see that she had no way out.

Her eyes were drawn back to the battle on the cliff. She watched as the knight fell to his knees and finally face forward onto the rocks. Immediately, she turned to face the dragon, her entire body racked with fear. She knew she faced a fate that death would be a release from.

At that instant, she heard her name called. Turning back, she saw the knight, in one last noble effort, rise to his feet and lift his sword. In the next moment, the sword was flying through the air toward her.

She watched the sword gliding to her and for a few seconds everything moved as if in slow motion. Even the leaves falling from the trees around her seemed to take an eternity to reach the ground. She knew that, in the end, her knight had saved her from the dragon.

She felt the sword as it penetrated her chest and heart, and thanked her God for her deliverance. As she sank to the ground, she called out almost inaudibly, "Thank you, Roland, my knight, my life."

***

Nevada, KS A young woman, identified as Shanna McGrey, was found dead today in her East Side apartment. A concerned former co-worker convinced police to investigate. She was discovered holding a large quartz crystal in one hand, while the other was wrapped around the hilt of an elaborate antique sword. The blade of which was buried in her chest.

Friends and neighbors told police that the woman's behavior had been strange for approximately the last month. Although other prints were found on the sword, due to circumstances found at the scene, the coroner had ruled her death a suicide.

CLEANLINESS IS NEXT TO ...

Maddie Maitland hated to clean. So much so that arguments over that one subject had broken up her marriage two years earlier. Since the day, Jake had moved out, Maddie had never so much lifted a broom in her house.

The vacuum cleaner had been the first to go, right after Jake. A young married woman at the factory had complained about the expense of a new cleaner, so Maddie had given hers to the young wife. One by one, the cleaning appliances had been given away, until now there was nothing left except an old dust mop hiding behind the refrigerator. Maddie had already forgotten its' existence.

Now she no longer even washed clothes. Preferring instead to just buying a couple pair of jeans, a few new shirts, underwear, and socks every payday. She had nothing else to spend her money on, the house and car were paid for, and her personal bills amounted to very little. In her own way, Maddie felt as if she were helping the local women's shelter by dropping off her dirty clothes about once a month.

She had stopped by the store on the way home and picked up her dinner; the latest and greatest frozen gourmet entree. Its' container would hit the floor when she was done. There was a movie on cable tonight that she had been waiting to see for months. Even though she had no romance in her own life, it did not keep her from living vicariously through others.

After eating her dinner, she poured herself an oversized glass of wine and popped a bag of microwave popcorn. Making herself comfortable on the sofa, she reached for the remote and settled in to watch her movie. Briefly, as it did occasionally, the thought crossed her mind that maybe she should hire a cleaning woman. "Too much trouble," she repeated to herself, completely dismissing the process as too complicated.

The movie had her so engrossed, she didn't notice the lightening in the distance. When the thunder boomed overhead loud and strong enough to shake the house, Maddie finally tore her eyes from the screen. Within moments, another crack of lightening lit up the night sky and at the same time, the power to the house came to a silent stop.

"Well, crap." Maddie exclaimed, feeling very pissed sitting in the dark. Allowing herself a few exasperated breaths, she finally got up and stumbled her way to bed. "Well, at least it's on again the day after tomorrow."

Stripping down, she climbed between the sheets of the bed. Feeling what felt like cracker or cookie crumbs, she made a mental note to herself to buy new sheets soon. Within moments she fell into a peaceful sleep amid the sounds of thunder and rain, and to the fireworks lighting up the sky.

The rain didn't stop the next day and the weatherman was calling for another round of storms for the evening. Maddie came home and repeated the events of the previous night. Curling up on the couch, she decided on reading a novel, instead of watching TV. Lighting a candle and placing it on the table beside the sofa, she figured she was ready if the storms were as severe.

This time she heard the approaching storm. She contemplated going on to bed, but instead just grabbed the quilt from the back of the couch and pulled it over her. Reaching for the jug of wine she had sat on the floor, she refilled her glass. It was Friday; after all, she didn't have to work tomorrow. A nice buzz and a good book felt like a good idea. After the third glass, she could feel herself snuggling in. Not much later, the lights once again lost power.

The dust bunny had sat on the electrical outlet behind the sofa for over five years. Slowly, from the neglect it had continued to grow, until it covered not only the outlet but also the light plug that was in it. As the storm raged outside, the surges through the outlet continued to energize the lamp repeatedly. Maddie was too soundly asleep to notice, not even rolling over until the sun from the window hit her in the face.

The dust bunny had moved while Maddie had slept. No longer on the outlet it now moved silently behind and under the sofa. No longer inanimate, it had no concept of being alive, only hunger. It had no idea of growth, yet as it moved it became larger, picking up the filth and dirt that had been quiet companions for years. As it grew, the need to feed became stronger, yet it had no realization of how to satisfy that need. It continued to move.

Maddie came in from her Saturday afternoon shopping trip and dumped the bags of purchases on the bed. She had splurged on this trip and had bought herself a good bottle of Irish whiskey.

Taking the foodstuff into the kitchen, she suddenly felt uncomfortable, as if she were being watched. Glancing around, she could see nothing different. Everything was just as she had left it earlier, yet she couldn't shake the feeling.

"Maybe a hot bath will help." She said aloud to herself.

Later, as she settled once again on the sofa for another attempt at the movie, she again had the feeling she wasn't alone. Looking around, she saw nothing and felt foolish.

"Must be getting paranoid in my old age", she said laughing as she poured herself a shot of the whiskey, "Maybe this will help."

She could feel the burn of the whiskey all the way to her belly and smiled. Very seldom did she allow herself the luxury of getting really drunk, but this was one night she had a plan to. As she waited for the movie to start, she had had several more shots and two large glasses of wine. By the time the movie was over, she had been asleep for over an hour.

The dust bunny moved. Seeing the quilt move on the back of the sofa, it attached itself to the edge. Moments later it was freed from its' prison and was covering the entire length of the woman along with the quilt. It could feel the movement of her chest moving up and down with her breath. Its' hunger intensified. Crawling closer to the warmth of her exhale, it knew what it needed to satisfy the craving. It moved closer and closer until it was totally covering the woman's mouth and nose. It grew stronger and stronger with each exhale. Then suddenly the breathing stopped,

yet the Dust Bunny felt as if it would
explode. Moments later, it ruptured into a thousand
pieces giving birth to others, all like itself. All had life;
all had hunger. They waited.

Five days later, the door burst open and a gust
of wind caught most of the offspring and carried them
out into the open air. Some attached themselves to the
clothing of the two men on the other side of the
threshold who went into sneezing fits as their nostrils
were filled with the escaping dust. Some just rode the
breeze until they found themselves on the ground
elsewhere.

The men standing were astonished. The entire
house was covered in filth. Small paths led from one
room to another. They found Maddie Maitland,
covered in dust, dead on the sofa. The police officer
called for the coroner and an ambulance.

The other man, who had been her supervisor at
work, could not believe his eyes.

"Who could live like this?" asked the cop.

"Good God, I've known this woman for almost
ten years she was such a neat freak at work."

UNRECALLED MEMORIES

She thought she knew her child so well. At least, she did up until the day he died. His brains bashed in from an aluminum baseball bat. The same bat, he had used moments earlier to beat his wife. After pitching the bat down in the hallway, he had sat down in his recliner and turned on the television. His seven year old son had crept up behind him and delivered the single lethal blow. The police said he probably hadn't known what hit him.

Now, Elin or Graham, had to reconsider everything. Young Tommy was for the time being, in her care. His mother was hospitalized in critical condition, no one sure whether she would live or not. Young Tommy, bruised and scarred from his father's repeated beatings, now had people eyeing him with suspicion. After all, young children just don't kill their parent.

Once again, the police were at her door.

"Mrs. Graham, I need to talk to the boy again."

"Haven't you talked to him enough?"

"We just have a few more questions."

"What more can he tell you. His mother told you everything before she went into the coma. He told you exactly what he did. What more can you want from that child?"

"The child killed his father, ma'am. We need to find out whether he planned to do it or not."

"Yes, the child killed his father. My son. The man who had just brutally beat the boy's mother in front of his eyes. The man who has left scars all over that little boy's body."

"I understand that this is difficult for you ma'am."

"What are you going to do, charge that poor child with murder?"

"No, ma'am. But there might be a manslaughter charge. We don't know yet."

They had talked to Tommy yet again. Elinor had hovered over the boy trying to protect him, while he repeated the same story he had already told a dozen times. All the while, Elinor wondered what had happened to her son.

Tom had grown up in a normal household and family. Father, Mother, two sisters. He had never been beaten, nor had ever received more than a swift swat on the behind when he had been a small child doing something unsafe like reaching for the hot stove.

In school, he had been well liked by his peers and his teachers, rarely getting into any trouble. He had graduated from both high school and college as valedictorian on his class. After college, he had started and still owned a prosperous computer business. Now he was dead at thirty.

When Elinor allowed herself to think, the one question that raged in her mind was, when had he changed into the monster that he was. Elinor had wanted to visit Sheri in the hospital and ask; now the young woman had slipped into a coma, so that door was closed to her.

Before the week was out, Elinor was being barraged by the media about the story. They were everywhere; calling on the telephone repeatedly and camping on her front yard. Twice a week she had to take Tommy to a psychologist and it was terrible for him. The reports would beat at the car windows and photograph him hunkered down in the front seat of the car.

Elinor had asked to police if there was not something she could do, but they had told her that it would die down and her best bet was to wait it out. What bothered her the most was the press and the chief district attorney all but calling her grandson a murderer.

The police showed up two weeks later with a warrant for the child's arrest. Manslaughter charges. The two cops were extremely apologetic and said they thought the whole thing was ridiculous. Elinor asked and was allowed to take Tommy to the police station herself; but not without an escort.

That night, Elinor granted her first interview with the press that had moved into her front yard.

"Is it true that your grandson has been charged with manslaughter?"

"It is. Although I cannot see how. That poor child's mother is almost dead in the hospital, and he himself has scars he will never outgrow."

"But the fact remains that he did kill his father, correct?"

"Yes, he did. But how anyone could say it was anything less than self-defense is beyond me."

"His father was your son, right? Did you know that he had such a violent nature?"

"No. It breaks my heart, but my son had become a monster and had I known it, I would have killed him myself."

"Do you think they will convict your grandson?"

"No, I've hired a good attorney and it is our feeling that this is just a ploy on the part of the district attorney because he is running for re-election. I feel sure when people hear all the facts, there will be an outcry in that child's favor."

With that, she turned around and entered the house. Tears were forming in her eyes. It just wasn't fair. That poor child in a jail cell tonight. Even though they told her it would have no bars, he was far away from those who loved him and had no way of reaching out. She could only imagine how afraid he must be.

The next day, Elinor went to the bank and mortgaged her house, using the money to pay Tommy's bond and pay the retainer for the lawyer. Supporters began lining the street she lived on, lighting candles in support for her grandchild. The trial was scheduled quickly, beginning in less than a month. As the days went on, more and more people lined the streets. Not all of them were kind.

The district attorney was on television several times during that time justifying his position. The last time he was on he had a tomato thrown in his face.

The night before the trial, the DA went to a convenience store to pick up a pack of smokes. He was shot dead during a holdup of the store.

The morning the trial was to begin, as Elinor was getting her grandson ready for court, the call came in.

"Mrs. Graham?"

"Yes, it is."

"This is Mary Shaman, John Rath's secretary. The district attorney was killed last night and the trial has been postponed. Mr. Rath said to tell you he would be by later to fill you in."

"Thank you," was all that Elinor could respond.

Was this nightmare never going to end? She thought to herself. How much longer could this go on. Hours later, there was a knock on the door.

"Hi, Elinor, can I come in?" Her lawyer, John Rath asked quietly.

Elinor opened the door fully.

"So what is going to happen now?" she asked.

"This is what I think will happen. First, we are going to petition the court to drop all charges. Then we wait. But I believe that the assistant district attorney will drop the charges. He has seen the public outcry, and he has no political motive at this moment for it to continue."

"So there is hope?"

"More than hope, I think. But still, I don't want you holding your breath. I do think this will work out, just never forget that sometimes life throws a curve at you."

Another week passed, and Tommy's mother died; never coming out of her coma. Tommy accepted it well. His life was already turned upside down. The psychologist said that it would all hit him later, after some type of normalcy returned to his life.

Yet another week passed in slow motion. The lawyer called and said all charges had been dropped. They could get on with their lives. The next day, Elinor called a real estate agent and the house was sold. Her and her grandson moved to a big city in California. No one knew them there or wanted to. They got on with living.

When Tommy was thirteen, he slapped his grandmother because she wouldn't give him cigarette money. Their relationship went downhill from there. When Tommy turned seventeen, he took a baseball bat and beat his grandmother to death. Her next to last thought was why? And before she took her last breath, she remembered her husband taking a belt to her son every time he didn't live up to his expectations. How could she have forgotten that? Maybe she did know her child, after all.

NO MORE, MAMA

The girl sat perched, on top of the wardrobe in the corner. She watched as the three men below took their turns raping her. Of course, it was only her conscious self that had deserted her body. If she had not have, the pain would have been too much for a twelve year old to bear.

It was not all necessarily the men's' fault. Her mother was the one who had sold her to them. Just as she had done with her older sister before her. But, Janie had left six months ago, just took off. The girl didn't believe that this was the first time for her. She felt that it had happened before, but her mind had closed off those memories to her.

Allowing her thoughts to wander, the girl tried not to hate her mother. Yet, she knew that it was impossible for her not too. If her mother needed the money for, food, for rent, for any real necessity, the girl might have even been able to understand. But for the price of a bottle of Mad Dog 20/20 was beyond the girl's comprehension. As the hate welled up inside of her, she thought of nothing else but revenge.

Morning came and the girl rose from her bed. She went into the bathroom and tried to doctor her wounds and scrub the filth she felt from her body. She knew her younger brother and sister had already left for school. Just as she knew her older brother and mother were passed out somewhere in the apartment, in an alcoholic haze.

As the hot water from the shower ran over her, she thought about her older brother. She blamed him almost as much as her mother. He was seventeen and shared their mother's bed whenever she could not find another man to take care of her drunken needs.

Everyone, the girl talked to, said the alcohol was to blame for her mothers' problems. But the girl knew that her mother was just a spiteful, selfish bitch. She didn't care how her own needs were met, just so long as they were. The girl wasn't sure how long she had hated the woman, but knew it had been as long as she could remember.

Now, she was going to put an end to it. Never again was her mother going to use her body to get what she wanted. And there was no way she was going to let her start on her little sister. Beth was only eight, she had enough heartaches just dealing with the beatings that her mother dished out regularly.

The girl emerged from the bath, clad only in an old shirt. Going into her room, she chose the cleanest of her clothes she could find. After dressing, she went into her closet and reached into the rat hole in the corner. Hoping it was not occupied, she fumbled around until her fingers closed on the small glass bottle. Pulling it out, she removed the lid. Using her pinkie finger, she tugged at the dollar bills that were inside. If her mother knew about this stash, chances were good her mother would beat her close to death.

Pushing the money deep into her jeans pocket, the girl silently made her way out of the apartment. She had a plan.

Taking the time to stop at the corner grocery to get change for bus fare, the girl ended up walking half way to town before the bus finally came along. Putting her change in the fare box, the girl found a seat near the rear of the bus. Usually she rode up front, where she could talk to the driver, but today, she needed quiet to think.

The idea had been playing around in her mind for the last several months. Ever since she had seen the book. It was a small volume, no more than a hundred pages. Yet for so little, the price seemed so expensive. It had taken the girl almost two months of can collecting to save the five dollars needed to buy it. But now she had it.

The bus pulled up in front of the Riviera Theater on Gay Street and the girl made her way to the exit.

"Bye, Sarah," the driver said, "next time, sit up front where we can talk."

"Maybe on the way back, Bobby." the girl replied with a smile.

Making her way through the back streets and alleys of the downtown district, she came to the bookstore. Really it was nothing more than a hole in the wall. It was dimly lit and most every book inside had layers of dust upon them. She wasn't sure why the old man let her sit in here and read, but he never complained about it. She supposed he took pity on her. Whatever it was, she didn't care as long as she could read.

As she walked up to the counter, Mr. Conner said, "Well hello there, Sarah. Skipping school again?"

"Just didn't feel up to it today, Mr. Conner. Sure am glad you let me hide out in her." she replied.

"From the looks of that bruise on the side of your face, it appears to me you're a lot safer in here." he said.

Not commenting on his remark, she asked, " Are you still holding that book for me, Mr. Conner?"

"Sure I am, Sarah. But what a nice kid like you needs with a book on demons and witchcraft is beyond me. Sure hope the situation at home isn't leading you into that kind of thinking." the old man said, shaking his head.

"Naw. It's just kind of fun to read about it, that's all. It's an interesting subject." she answered.

Taking the bills from her pocket, she handed the money to the old man. Placing the book in a paper sack, he passed it over the counter to her.

"Well, gotta run now, Mr. Conner. Maybe I'll see you next week sometime. And, oh, thanks. For holding the book and all."

Sarah left the store and almost ran back to the main street of town. She couldn't wait to find a quiet place to read and put her plan into action.

Boarding a bus to Magnolia Avenue, she thought she would find the isolation she needed at the old amusement park. This time of year, the place would be deserted. Once there, she walked the fence line until she found a hole large enough to crawl through. Watching for the security guard, she made her way to the game booths. She knew if she climbed into one, she would not be noticed. Finding her spot, she sat down and began to read. An hour later, she came to the passage that had first caught her attention in the bookstore.

"To cause death to come to greet your enemy, you must first evoke the powers of darkness to aide you."

Reading on, Sarah saw that the ceremony was simple. No black candles or pentagrams or anything else that TV had taught her to associate with witchcraft. All it took was a few simple words and a firm belief that it would work. Sarah knew she could do both. All she had to do now, was wait until dark.

Continuing to read, she waited till the shadows made it impossible. Darkness didn't scare her, except when she was locked in the closet. She had already memorized the words of the chant. As soon as the darkness was complete, she closed her eyes and began uttering the words. "Suma, Saktara, Ismah, Da." Over and over she chanted, rocking on her ankles beneath her.

Thoughts and images flew through her young mind. Suddenly, she was once again leaving her body and floating through space. She found herself outside her own apartment door. She knew she had no need to open it and just drifted through. Inside she saw what she had invited with her words.

The demon stood over her brother's body. Her mother lay beside him in the bed. Both were naked. Her mother's head was twisted on her neck in a way that Sarah knew she could not be alive. Her brother had his fist around the handle of a butcher knife, buried in his chest.

"Have I done well, Mistress?" the creature asked.

Sarah looked directly at him now, but felt no fear. The demon was short and squat. His skin was scaly looking, like a lizard. In fact, that's what he reminded the girl of; a reptile standing on its hind feet. He had bulging eyes, with no lids, and his tongue darted in and out so fast that she wondered how he could talk.

"You've done great. Thank you. My other brother and sister, you didn't hurt them, did you?" she asked.

"No, Mistress, they are asleep in the other room. I made no noise. They are having pleasant dreams." the demon responded. "If that is all, I will leave now. Remember, I am always here to serve you."

Immediately the creature vanished and Sarah found herself back at the carnival booth. Replacing the book back in the paper sack, she hid it behind the curtains of her hiding place. She knew it would not do to go home with it tonight. She would come back for it later.

Arriving home, she found everything as she had already seen it. Gently waking her brother and sister, she led them out and up the stairs to the apartment above. Neighbors called the police. Knowing the abuse the girl had suffered, no one was surprised when she didn't cry.

PARANOIA

She was a timid woman. Her only real joy in life was her cello. Even that could not sustain her in the way she wished. Forced by circumstances, she taught young children her art. She had discovered early in life there were only so many symphonies. Although she was very, very good, others who were better took those few jobs.

Later in life, she would find that teaching children during the day had worked out well for her. Being withdrawn, she had had few dates in her life. She was only thirty-five, but even at that age, her prospects for marriage were slim. Most men found her to be not just shy, but also extremely flaky. Inevitability though, her paranoia would leave a man shaking his head, wondering why he was wasting time with her.

She was afraid of many everyday occurrences: crowded places (a lunatic could be there with a gun), city parks and parking lots (everyone knows rapists wait there), and dogs (they attack, disfigure and maim). I could go on and on. As she would watch the nightly news, her list would grow.

Every small sound startled her. She rarely ventured out after dark and when she did, she was always watching over her shoulder. Her car was equipped with a burglar alarm and a searchlight. Her neighbors, me included, would know she was home by the light shining in our windows as she projected the beam over the entire area surrounding the front of her house.

Once inside her home, the number of visible locks at once struck people. Every window had at least two, with bars covering them besides. Huge bar locks braced both front and rear doors. Even the interior doors were furnished with double key locks. The key to which she wore on a chain around her neck. There was also a very sophisticated alarm system involving motion detectors.

For me, her closest neighbor, she was a source of ridicule. I asked her once why she was so careful; what had happened that had made her afraid to live life. She responded that it was a cruel world and that someone was always out there waiting to catch a person off-guard. Did some terrible tragedy occur to her at some time? No, she had replied, but you have to be ready for it when it did. At least that was her explanation for her situation. So I watched her comings and goings with a hint of comic interest. Only at night would I rage when her damn searchlight would blare into my bedroom window, blazing light through my sleeping eyelids, waking me with a start.

As I lay in my bed, after one of the incidents, I would think to myself that one of these days, her imagined bogeymen were going to come to get her. After all, it was people like her that attracted that sort of thing. I believed that if a person dwelled on thought of doom and destruction, then they were going to come true for them.

One night, after being woke up for the umpteenth time by her light, I thought I heard something jump in the bushes by my house. She had begged me many times to cut the shrubs back or better yet, take them out altogether. I had refused. I liked my bushes, and maybe if I admitted it, I got a little sadistic satisfaction out of the fact that they were a source of concern for her.

I lay there, listening to see if I heard anything else. A few moments later, I heard a scratching. It sounded like it was at her front door. Thinking to myself that it must be her cat, I thought nothing more about it. Rolling over, I went back to sleep.

I wasn't asleep very long, when I heard her scream. Jumping out of bed, trying to slide into a pair of jeans and a shirt, I felt I should go investigate. After all, I didn't want to call the police out if she really wasn't in trouble. She called in enough false alarms on her own. Going out the front door, I decided to just peek in the windows and see if anything was happening.

Starting at her front window, I carefully made my way around her house until I was looking in her kitchen. What I saw there made me realize that I should have called the police before coming over. If I told them now what I saw, there was no way they would believe me, yet I knew I couldn't handle this myself. Running back to my own house, I dialed 911. Playing it smart, I just reported a break-in, no more.

The call made, I stood and debated going back. My logical mind refused to believe what I had seen. A sense of duty and morbid curiosity took me back to her kitchen window. I yelled out asking if she was all right. In response, I heard only terrified pleas for help. Gathering every ounce of courage I possessed, I forced myself to look again into the window.

Pressed against the far kitchen wall, she stood holding a meat cleaver, her eyes wide with terror. Straining to see what she was focused on, my eyes went to the floor. There, standing two or three feet away from her, were two tiny creatures.

They were no more than twelve inches tall, and looked much like a small dog, standing up on their hind legs. Only these were not dogs. These beings were alien, straight from a nightmare. Moving about upright, they carried what appeared to be small guns, which they shot at her constantly. From her waist down, small wounds were bleeding profusely. Blood covered her entire lower body. That alone was enough to make me nauseous. But when I saw their faces, my blood ran ice cold.

Snout-like with huge mouths, filled with large sharp pointed incisors. Long dark tongues darted rapidly in and out through their fangs. That is the only way I can think of to describe those teeth. Eyes blazing green, in red-rimmed drooping eyelids, their entire faces were covered in fur-like hair.

In my terror, I remembered the old werewolf movies I had seen on the late show. Somehow, I knew that even Hollywood could not come up with something this horrible. These miniature werewolves made me believe in all that is evil. Dashing about the woman, they continued to shoot. Watching them, black tongues licking their lips in anticipation, I knew without a doubt, they were only waiting for her to fall. Once she hit the floor, their feast would begin.

Somewhere in my brain, the sane part wondered where the police were. How long ago had I called them? If only there was something else I could do, but the house was locked up too tight. The bars covering the windows prevented breaking the glass to enter. I could only stand and watch until the police arrived. They would probably have to shoot the locks on the doors to gain entrance. I could only hope they would arrive in time.

By now, her eyes had begun to glaze over. I had doubts about whether or not she was coherent any longer. Her own animal instincts for survival kept her from giving up. As if they could sense her resolve, they advanced, making their shots hit her upper body.

As the small beasts closed in, she began making small jabs toward them with the cleaver. She was reaching nowhere near them. Her efforts were in vain. Suddenly, her eyes cleared and were darting around searching for a means of escape. There was none. I could imagine her cursing the locks that now held her prisoner. She had no way out; I had no way in.

I felt her eyes meet mine in a silent plea. Bound by the horror I was witnessing, I was frozen in place. I could not force my body to move, it was completely unresponsive.

Moments later, I became aware of another presence. Terrified, I slowly turned my head, seeing only a gun pointed at my left temple. In that instant, I almost laughed aloud in relief. The gun was held, not by another beast, but by a young policeman. Without a word, I pointed to the window. Not taking his gun off of me, the youthful rookie peered through the glass. An instant later, the gun fell to the grass and a wet stain began to form on his trousers.

Several minutes passed before he began to recover. Telling me he had to call for back up, he left me alone once again. When he returned, he retrieved his gun from where it had fallen. The blank expression remained on his face. We continued our lookout at the window.

In a very subdued whisper, he asked, "Do you think bullets will kill them?"

"I don't know." I replied shaking my head.

Taking aim, he fired at the closer of the two beasts. Amid the shattering glass, I ducked to avoid being hit by the shards. The cop, still in firing position, was mumbling that he had hit the beast. Why wasn't it dead? Taking aim once more, he fired again, then again, until his gun was empty. The pitiful young man beside me was now muttering incoherently. I knew, just from looking at his face, he had lost his mind.

Seconds later, a very bright light had us in its beam. Two officers, guns in hand, were approaching us from the street. I was still in my crouching position under the window. I put my finger to my lips, hoping to silence them until they discovered what they were up against. In a booming voice, one of the two informed me the house was surrounded. Calmly, I told them it was useless. One glance in the window, confirmed for them what I meant.

Other officers came from around the house and joined us at our window vigil. Like the first, they stood spellbound in horror at what they were witnessing. Minutes passed, still no one moved, no one talked. All eyes remained fixed on the beasts and woman.

The silence was broken when someone behind me asked,

"What the hell are they?"

The only answer came from the rookie.

"They don't die. I shot them, but they don't die. They don't die."

I thought someone should lead him away. No one did, as it became obvious to us all that the woman could take no more. As her back began sliding down the kitchen wall, she looked toward the group assembled. With utter helplessness in her eyes, she mouthed the words "Shoot Me!"

Her body hit the floor and the beasts were upon her instantly. Chewing and ripping the meat and flesh from her legs, the creatures were lost in a feeding frenzy. The woman had not lost consciousness yet and most of us at the window were turning away trying to shield ourselves from the ghastly scene we had just viewed.

From beside me, a gruff looking, mature officer raised his gun. A second later she was dead. Another moment or two and nothing was left of her from neck down except sinew and bone. The beasts were missing too. It was as if they had vanished into the vapors.

* * *

Now, a month later, the case is closed. Official verdict: murder and mutilation by person or persons' unknown. Police response too slow and the perpetrators already vacated from the scene. No one questioned this report, but an investigation has been launched on how to speed police response time. The rookie's rambling's about werewolves and miniature guns, was taken as just that. It was felt that the young officer became mentally unhinged by the brutality of what he discovered answering the call.

For my part, I was told to keep my mouth shut or I would be joining him at the state hospital. I readily agreed, after all, no one would believe me anyway.

Sleep has not come easy this last month. Nightmares plague me. From them, I now understand what happened next door. Because of that knowledge, I have given up my office job and work at home. Daytime is the only time I can sleep. In my dreams, enormous fanged snakes chase me. I awake in absolute panic, cold sweat pouring from my body.

I know, without a doubt, that those creatures came from her imagination. Forming from what she loathed the most. Gaining strength by terrorizing her according to one of her worst fears: being attacked and destroyed by a pack of wild dogs. Her biggest mistake was that her motion detectors were installed too high. At a two-foot level, the beasts only had to make themselves smaller to beat her security system.

I still have no heavy locks on my doors or windows. I saw how that defeated her. But, the man was here today installing my detectors. He looked at me, like I was off in the head when I gave him my instructions. My order was simple; I wanted them

spaced at half-foot intervals, starting at floor level
continuing to the ceiling, throughout the
house. Nothing can move now, without the alarm
sounding.

Tonight I sit motionless in my chair, television
on low, with a shotgun across my lap. I know that if I
let my guard down, even for an instant, they will
come. My fears will reach out for me as surely as they
did for her. It's only a matter of time.

PRACTICAL JOKE

The chicken king was taking a bubble bath during the middle of a war. It wasn't a war that involved soldiers, only two natural born leaders. The explosion of tempers was erupting from his wife and teenaged daughter. Both had wills of iron and lately seemed to be at odds over everything from the dinner menu to boyfriends.

He could hear the mouse skittering behind the shower wall. It almost made him smile. This one tiny creature was the subject of the battle going on outside the hallway door.

"You can't kill it Mom. It's just an innocent creature."

Julie was saying in a matter of fact tone. Equal in tone, was his wife's reply, "I am not going to have unwanted four legged creatures in this house. Do you understand me Julie? That mouse is dead."

"Well, at least let me trap it and return it to the outside." The chicken king could hear the pleading in his daughter's voice.

"Dead, Julie. The mouse is dead."

"You're no better than a murderer, Mom."

"Where there is one, there are more. Just as soon as your father is out of the bath, I'm putting down poison."

"I hate you, Mother."

"I love you Julie." He smiled again, that had been Gwen's standard reply since Julie had first uttered the words at age three.

John Graham, the chicken king, came up with a plan. He was known throughout the state as the best chicken farmer in the business. Growing chickens quickly for production had earned him numerous awards from the nation's top producer. Getting up from the tub slowly, he wrapped a towel around his large frame. If nothing else, his wife would get her way and the mouse would be dead. If what he was thinking worked both his wife and daughter would freak and that would be good for a laugh or two with the guys down at the bar. It was worth a try.

True to her word, Gwen laid out the mouse poison as soon as John disappeared into the bedroom to get dressed.

A few minutes later, he emerged in work clothes. Seeing his wife in the recliner reading a magazine, he kissed her on the forehead.

"I'm going out to check on the chickens. Wanna come?" He knew full well she wouldn't. As much as she liked spending the money they made, she hated the source.

"That's ok." She said with a smile.

John was out the door and on the way to the first of the huge chicken houses. The first house held a storage room on one end and that was where his feet were heading. Inside the room, he scanned the shelves until he spotted what he was looking for. Pulling down the large bag, he grabbed a handful of the contents and stuffed his hand into his pocket. Replacing the bag on the shelf, he headed back to the house.

Inside the bathroom, he took the small box of poison and dumped it into his empty pocket. Taking the contents from his other pocket, he refilled the small box and sat it on the floor. "Here's hoping," he thought to himself. He was whistling as he left the bathroom.

For several days, the mouse continued to make its presence known. Gwen had remarked that there had to be more than one for as much noise as it was making. At dinner, it had once again become an issue.

"Your poison isn't working Mom." Julie said.

"I'm guessing there's more than one. I checked the poison and it is being eaten. So I know there is at least one dead mouse."

"That is so gross. You are so cruel, Mom."

"You wouldn't think so if they were scurrying across your bed."

The argument continued for several more minutes about to erupt into a full-fledged cat fight between wife and daughter. The chicken king stepped in, "The poison is out, the mice are eating it, and it is a done deal. I don't want to hear any more about it at the dinner table."

"You're as bad as she is Daddy." Julie came back with, as she skid her chair across the hardwood floor. "I can't wait to get out of here." She screamed as she went through the door of the dining room.

Ouch. That one hurt, thought John. It would serve her right if a mouse did scurry across her bed. Just before he dropped off to sleep that night he could hear that the mice had made it to the attic. He imagined that they must be getting bigger if he could hear them up there. He went to sleep smiling.

Two nights later, Gwen and he were awakened by Julie's screams. Rushing into her room, they found their daughter hysterical. She was babbling between tears about a large rat being on her chest. Gwen dismissed it as a dream, John had to wonder. There was no question of going back to sleep tonight, Julie would let neither of them out of her sight. They finally decided to go on down to the kitchen for breakfast as it would be daylight soon. John was ready for a cup of coffee anyway. As bright sunshine filled the kitchen, Julie finally began to calm down. Once he felt that she would be all right with just Gwen, John grabbed a flashlight and headed for the attic. Shining the light around, he looked for any sign of the noises he had been hearing for several nights. He saw nothing.

He went down to the bathroom and checked the poison box. Half full. The mice hadn't eaten enough to cause any changes. Shrugging he headed out to the chicken houses for his daily chores. Days passed and he forgot about it all. Gwen continued to complain about hearing the mice and Julie continued to defend the "innocent" creatures, blaming her nightmare on her mother for planting the idea in her head.

A month later, they were once again awakened by Julie's screams, coming from the upstairs bath. Gwen raced to the room using the hallway light to guide her. John followed and flipped the light switch on. Pure fear crept up the back of his neck as he surveyed the room. Gwen and Julie were both in the tub, the floor covered by hundreds of large mice. Not rats, but mice large enough to battle a sewer rat with ease. He tried to remain calm.

"Gwen, Julie, move slowly over here." He said, his voice barely a whisper.

"I can't." Came his daughters reply.

"You have to, Julie. Come on, we can do this." Gwen said, taking her daughter by the hand and trying to pull her up.

John watched in horror as the mice advanced clamored on top of each other, getting closer and closer to the top of the tub.

"You have to move now!"

It was too late. The mice had scrambled into the tub, cloaking the two women in various shades of brown fur. John could hear their screams as they were being bit, yet he could not force himself to move. When he finally did, it was toward his own bedroom. Their screams followed him. Coming back to the doorway, he aimed the shotgun and fired. As fast as he could load, he fired the double-barreled shotgun again and again.

He could not look at his wife and daughter. He knew they were dead. He had killed them. He could hear sirens approaching. He heard the banging on the door and it being busted in. He could only stand at the bathroom door with the shotgun in his hand.

The police were in the hall, guns drawn. Talking to him. He could not hear the words they were saying. He began, "It was just a joke, a practical joke. They were arguing about the mice. I fed them growth hormone pellets, you know the stuff I feed the chickens to make them grow faster. I didn't know, I didn't know"

Tears streaming down his cheeks, John Graham the chicken king, his insanity apparent, placed the barrel of the shotgun in his mouth. "I'm sorry." He said and pulled the trigger.

The two cops winced at the sound of the blast. Frozen momentarily by what they had just witnessed, neither moved; they only stared in disbelief. Out of the bathroom poured the mice. They thronged over the remains of John Graham's body. Both men fled.

Later, in a bar, a very drunk policeman was telling the story to anyone who would listen.

"I swear, man, you could see those mice growing as they ate."

THE SINKHOLE

If Tommy hadn't felt so dejected, the trouble might not have started at all. As it was, he was only trying to escape. You ask, what does a twelve year old kid have to escape from? Tommy called it the do's and don'ts.

He had just got home from school and immediately it began. His Mama was the doer; do this Tommy, do that Tommy. His Poppa, the don'ter; don't do this Tommy, don't do that Tommy. It was always something from one of them. As soon as supper was over and he had taken all the nagging he could stand, he headed out the back door.

The child had no plans to go to the sinkhole, he just kind of ended up there. Inside his head, he could hear his father's voice, "Don't go near the sinkhole son. It's a dangerous place. People have been killed there."

The sinkhole was like a large crater. It sat in the center of a block, with about twenty houses backed up to it. A few years ago, the city had become concerned because after it rained, it held back up water and became swampy. Some brilliant engineer decided if they enlarged the cave opening, then the water would drain off faster. The city came in with bulldozers and backhoes and installed a metal culvert through the mouth of the cave.

Unfortunately, that didn't work. The problem got worse. It didn't drain at all. The first spring after they did the work, it rained hard for a couple of days. By the time it had ended, all you could see of some houses were the rooftops. The city had to bring in big pumper trucks and pump the water blocks away to drainage ditches. The people who owned the houses started suing the city, claiming they had caused the problem, so they could buy them out.

Anyhow, there he was, kicking around the culvert. Picking up a heavy stick, Tommy started banging it against the metal sides. Much to chicken to go in very far, he always wondered what it was like inside the cave. Last year, some guy from the city was down here poking around, and he died. They said he lost his footing. But whatever, the guy was dead.

If he had been paying more attention, he would have heard the punks approaching. By the time he realized it, they were standing at the mouth of the opening.

"Hey, what have we found here? Thought we told you to stay away, Shultz." said the one on the right, standing with his arms folded across his chest. He had a cigarette dangling from the corner of his mouth, and both had packs rolled in the sleeves of their tee shirts. His partner was in an almost identical pose, except one hand circled the neck of a beer bottle.

Trying desperately not to show his fear, Tommy started slowly backing into the cave. Anyone with a little sense was afraid of this place, so Tommy was positive they wouldn't follow him in.

"Shultz, get you skinny little ass back out here. If we have to come in there after you, you're going to be crawling home to Mommy, instead of walking." one of them said.

To Tommy, the darkness came quickly. He didn't think he had come in this far. The difference in temperature, was like going into an air-conditioned house on a hot, humid day.

It was obvious Tommy wasn't aware that he was still backing up. At least until he realized, that although he could still hear them yelling, he could not understand what they were saying.

Digging into his pockets, he wished that his mother hadn't made him change jeans that morning. He had a pack of matches in the pocket of the other pair. Trying a trick his father had taught him, he closed his eyes tight, and hoped when he opened them his eyes would be adjusted to the darkness. Re-opening his eyes, he could see a little better. Just a bit, but it helped. Looking around, he could make out a dim light coming from one of the tunnels. Wishful thinking and a silent prayer, had him hoping it was another way out. Putting his hand against the side of the cave, he started toward the light.

The path below made a crunching sound as he walked. He was almost glad he didn't have better light. Maybe it was better not to know what was down there. Getting closer to the source of the light, he could hear voices. Thinking it was the two bullies from the culvert, he tried to pick his way faster down the tunnel. Although the light was getting better, he was too busy watching behind him to notice the drop off as he approached it.

Feeling his feet slide out from beneath him, he went butt first into a room. In disbelief, he saw that it was furnished. Not like the furniture in any normal house, but some roughly hewn pieces that were shaped like a table and chairs. Was someone living down here, and if so, why? Standing up and brushing off the seat of his pants, childhood curiosity drew him further into the room.

Not knowing now which direction to watch, he decided he had more to fear from what was down here. Trying to keep along the side of the walls, slowing inching his way around the room, he came to another opening. There was another room similar in size to the first. This one had a couple of makeshift beds and a small torch hanging on the wall.

The logical part of his brain was telling him to run, yet part of him wanted to see who or what was living down here. Spotting the next opening, he made his way toward it. Peeking around the corner, his inquisitiveness was satisfied, as he saw the occupants of the cave.

His rational self was saying that this was not possible. From the few short seconds he had looked, they looked like people. They were standing straight and they had facial features that resembled humans, but they did not have any eyes the boy could see. They wore no clothing, as they had hair covering their entire bodies.

Not believing, Tommy had to look again. Taking a deep breath and holding it, he looked once again around the corner. He found he was unable to stop staring at them. They had to be human, at least, in some sense of the word. They were talking, but not in any recognizable language. The boy stood there spellbound, when suddenly he could hear the panic rise in their voices. They had spotted him.

In the boys' mind, it felt like forever before he could get his legs to move. Running and stumbling, he headed back the way he had come. He didn't have to turn and look. He was aware that they were right behind him. The chattering noises they were making sent chills through his young body.

So close he could swear he felt their breath on his back, he found his way back to the culvert. Running into the daylight, he realized the two punks were still there waiting. Screaming at them to run, he knocked one down as he pushed through them and headed for the street. Not until Tommy reached the road did he foolishly turn and look back.

The three largest creatures emerged out of the culvert. The two punks were still shouting obscenities at him. By the time they understood the danger, it was too late. The boy stood and watched as the monsters ripped the heads off the older boys. Two other creatures emerged and the five of then picked up the bodies and headed back into the cave. The boy lost what was left of his dinner as the smallest one began chewing on an arm.

Terrified, he ran home. Taking the stairs two at a time, he slammed the bedroom door behind him. Later, when his mother came up to check on him, he assured her he was fine. He knew, with a new found maturity, he couldn't tell anyone what he had just witnessed. No one would believe, they would say it was all his imagination.

The following night his father read in the paper how two teenagers had disappeared. It was assumed that they had just run away. His mother made the comment that if Tommy didn't start shaping up, he was going to turn into a hoodlum just like them. If only they knew the truth, he thought.

As the days passed, several other people who lived around the sinkhole turned up missing. No one connected the two together. Two weeks later, the spring rains began. The sinkhole flooded and no one else vanished. The boy convinced himself that the creatures were dead.

The city eventually bought out all the property owners and erected a tall security fence around the sinkhole. Life went on in the neighborhood. Most people forgot about the kids and others who had disappeared. For months, the boy was plagued by nightmare he refused to discuss. A year later, the family moved to another city and the child rested a little easier. But he never forgot.

* * *

Today, twenty years later, Tom Shultz went back. Standing at the fence and looking into the culvert, he knows that they are still there. He knows too, that one day they will come out again. The man bowed his head and prayed that the fence, meant to keep people out, would keep the creatures in.

SUDDENLY SOBER

I open my eyes and see the pillow poised over my face. Yet in my drunken state, I am helpless to struggle, unable to stop what I know is inevitable. I can only hope my murderer will be swift and merciful.

The pillow moves closer, the hands holding it gripping the edges tightly, firmly, white knuckled. I am still unable to fight my destiny. Instead I think about my life and what I have done with it. Enough of that, I have accomplished nothing. I think about my children, the ones I never should have had. I think about all the trouble they have caused, simply by being in my life. I think of how I have made them pay for the misery they have brought to me.

My two boys are next to useless. They can't even steal enough food to keep me fed, let alone themselves. All the boys have been good for is sexual satisfaction, but really, as far as lovers go, they were lousy in bed. I pity the women they try to make love too.

The girls, well at least they are easier to keep in line. They earn their keep, sleeping with the men who bring me my liquor. They whine and bitch about it, but in the end they do it, even if I have to tie them to the bed. What choice do they have, after all I am their mother, they have to do what I say, don't they?

I open my eyes because I can feel the pillow. I raise my hand and try to push it away. For just a moment I see the face of the one holding it. It is my oldest son. The ungrateful bastard. I brought him into this world and this is how he repays me?

I push at the pillow once more, trying to see who else is in the room. I see all my children. Their eyes are so cold. Emotionless. I don't understand. Why are they doing this to me?

The pillow is now pressed against my face. I am struggling to breathe. I don't have the energy or even the inclination to fight. My son is strong. For some reason, that surprises me. No matter, I can feel the life leaving my body. I'm getting weaker. I need a drink. Just to take the edge off. Wait a minute, no I don't. Suddenly, I can think clearly.

Oh, God, why are they doing this to me?

THE CHANGLINGS

The dreams haunted her day and night. Evil twisted thoughts that no mother should have. She no longer knew her children. They had become unknown aliens who lived in her house, ate her food and demanded more and more of her energy.

When her son had turned fifteen the dreams began. At first, only occasionally and then more frequent as the next year went by. When her daughter turned fifteen, they came more rapidly, now to the point where they were an every night occurrence.

In those dreams, her precious children were no longer humans. Only demons hiding behind the masks of her children's faces. Abigail, Abbi to her friends, Anderson believed now she was losing her mind. Her interactions with her teens had become strained. Once a loving mother, she could hardly bare to speak to them now. When she did, she could hear the fear in her voice and it was obvious that they could too. The two children played on that fear.

Her son had quit school over six months earlier and now spent his days eating, listening to rock music and ordering his mother to do this or that for him. The evil emanating from his eyes made it impossible for Abbi to refuse.

Her daughter no longer thought of anything but good times and parties. She was still in school for the moment, but the last time Abbi had told her no, she had disappeared for five days. She came back home, yet held her mother hostage with the words "I'll just do it again" if anything happened to displease her.

Instead of love for her children, Abbi was now counting down the days until each one, in their turn, celebrated their eighteenth birthday and she would no longer be responsible for them. Abbi only hoped she could hold on to her sanity that long.

The week before Halloween, the children informed her that they were having a party.

"This is what we need, get it." Andrew said, handing her a long list.

"I can't afford all this stuff." Abbi had protested.

"That's not my problem. If you love us, you will find a way, Mother." had been his response.

Two days later, her daughter had given her another list. On it were items Abbi had never allowed in her home.

"Shari, you know I don't allow alcohol here." She had said, reading over the list.

"My friends won't come unless we have it. And I am not losing friends over one of your silly rules." Sheri's tone said that no matter what; the booze would be at the party.

That night Abbi had the worse dream yet. In it she had been awakened from sleep by two demons standing over her bed, chanting. When she opened her eyes in the dream, she saw what her children were. Abbi had shrunk down in the bed with fear. The larger of the two creatures reached out and gripped her shoulders with scaly talon like hands. Holding her pinned to the bed, the other being spoke, "You will do as your children wish. You have no choice. If you do not, you will find that your life has been very easy up until now."

The creature licked its' lips, the look in its' eyes lustful and menacing.

"I promise we can do much worse to you than just dreams." The glee resonated in its' deep guttural voice.

Abbi woke up then, a cold sweat pouring from her body. What was going on, she thought to herself, where are these dreams coming from? Looking over at the clock, she saw that it was five am. There was no use trying to go to work today, she was too shaken to concentrate, even though her factory job of assembling prongs on cord, was something she could do by rote. She had lost so much work in the last few months that she expected to be fired at any moment. Only her seniority had protected her job this long.

Deciding to take a hot shower, Abbi climbed out of bed. In her mind she was grateful it was so early, her children never stirred this early. She had over an hour before Sheri would get up for school, if she decided to go. An hour several cups of coffee later, she still had not heard the alarm clock from the room down the hall. Abbi knew she now had at least three hours of peace and quiet, before either of them stirred.

Abbi was not a praying woman, yet she found herself on her knees beside her bed as she went in her room to get dressed for the day.

"Please God, help me. I don't know what is
going on. Please, God."

The tears began to flow. Abbi wasn't sure how
long she stayed there repeating herself, but finally she
pushed herself up to her feet. Walking into the closet,
she grabbed the first pair of jeans and a sweatshirt that
she saw. Grabbing her purse, she headed for the front
door. She was not going to stay in this house with the
two of them today. Passing the side table in the
hallway, she spotted their lists. Without thinking, she
picked them up and shoved them into her purse, then
went out the door. Seven hours later, she returned to
the house.

"Where have you been?" Andy confronted her
the moment she opened the door. "I called work and
they said you didn't show up today."

"I took the day off." Abbi felt like a child again,
being questioned by her parents instead of the other
way around.

"Well, I guess you have every day off
now. They told me to tell you to pick up you
check. Good going Mom. Now you have no income."

"She can file for unemployment and there's
always Dad's child support." Sheri chimed in. "There
will be plenty of money, now that she won't be out
there wasting it on lunch and clothes."

"Did you at least pick up the stuff on our lists,
while you were out lazing the day away?" Andy asked.

"It's in the trunk of the car." Abbi replied,
resignation hanging heavy in her voice.

"Oh, I need another hundred dollars." Sheri said.

"I don't have a hundred dollars." Abbi replied.

"Sure you do." Sheri said, grabbing the purse from Abbi's hands.

"What a liar." The young girl said, withdrawing all the cash out of the billfold.

For the next three days before the party Abbi walked around mostly in a daze. She tried to close her mind off to everything. Halloween arrived and her house was filled with teenagers. She retreated to her room. Four and a half hours later, she woke to a quieter house. She could hear soft mumbled conversation coming from the living room and decided to go see who was still up.

Rounding the corner to the living room, she saw that every available space was taken up with the demon like creatures of her dreams.

"Hello, Abbi. Sleep well? We've been waiting for you."

Abbi could only stare. She wanted to scream but found she had no voice. The creature closest to her rose from the chair, and grabbing her pushed her into in.

"You see Abbi, we are no dream. We are your children and your neighbor's children."

"How?" she managed to squeak out the word.

"Children today. They are so easy to enter. So selfish and self-absorbed. They want it all and they want it now. It is so easy for them to trade their soul for the things they feel they deserve."

"But . . ."

"Did they not make you feel that no matter what you did, it was never enough? Sure they did. That was all it took. A selfish desire for more. Once upon a time, we had so few hosts. Children were different then. They respected their parents. Now, there are so many."

Another creature opened their mouth and began speaking,

"Fifteen is such a magical age. One foot in childhood, the other in adulthood. It is that age where it is easy for us. Their longings allow us a foothold, when they get a taste of what we can give them, they only want more."

"So you see, Abbi, you are stuck with us. At least a few more years. We need you. And you will be there for us because you have no choice. We control you. Do you understand what we are saying to you, Abbi?"

Abbi was no longer listening; her mind, gone forever, to somewhere safe. Away from the terror in her living room, away from the body she once called her own.

THE FAN

Soon. Carin Thompson turned the folded piece of paper over, searching for anything else. Nothing. Just one word. Soon. She looked again at the envelope that it had arrived in. Nothing there either except her name and address neatly printed in block letters. Almost as if stenciled. No return, even the postmark was unreadable. Deciding it was trash; she threw it away and forgot about it. At least until the next one came.

I am coming. Like the one before, nothing else. Carin wondered which of her friends was pulling a prank. This would be like one of them. After all, no one else had her address. Even her bills did not come here, all going to a post office box. That was the first thing she had learned after her first novel was published. Fans, as much as you enjoy having them, can be very annoying when they invade your personal life. Looking back at the three words, her gut tightened. Instinct told her that maybe this was not a friend. She took the letter and put it into a manila folder. She would wait and see what happened.

The time is near. As Carin looked at this one, her first thought was that maybe some local Jesus freak was harassing her. After all, the locals would know her address. For all she knew, it could be the postman himself. Her instincts once again told her this wasn't the case, yet she put this one with the previous one in the folder and dismissed it from her mind.

Almost there. Carin, for the first time felt threatened. Maybe it was time to call the sheriff. But what could she tell him? There had been no threats

made. Just these notes. Not wanting to appear like a
silly woman to the redneck locals, she decided to wait.

I am watching you. The hair on the back of her
neck stood on end. Compulsion caused her to look
around. She saw nothing. Once again, she considered
calling the sheriff; once again she decided to wait.

I can see you. Now there was no
question. Reaching for the phone she called. Several
hours later, she felt foolish. The sheriff had made a
pointed effort to show her how irrational she was
being. He believed there was no danger. Nothing more
than a prank. He had even hinted that she was making
everything up.

I am here. The words were written on the
fogged up mirror as she stepped out of the hot shower.

THE TREE PEOPLE

I remember living in the woods. This recollection must be an echo from a distant past. It is a scant memory, to my mind all I see are massive tree's blocking out any hope of sunlight.

The place we called home was dug out of the trunk of one of the enormous trees. There was only room to sleep; yet it did provide shelter from the winter snow and ice. Leaves made up my bedding and at night I would bury myself in them in a useless attempt to keep warm.

During the day, we ventured out, searching for berries in the spring and summer and nuts in the fall and winter. Occasionally someone would snare a bird or a rabbit. We would eat it raw as a fire could destroy the woods we were hidden in.

From what we were hiding, I do not know. Yet we moved through the woods silently, ever watchful for movement in the forest that surrounded us.

Fear seemed to be the basic motivation in all we did. Always talking in hushed whispers when words were necessary. Mostly we had signs and gestures to communicate our thoughts to others. Our world was a quiet one. No sounds of laughter. No sounds of crying. But, always the watching. Always someone was watching.

Somewhere deep in my mind I understood it could not last. Someone would slip and give us away. Tension can only be bound so tight and then it explodes. I was glad it was not me.

When it did happen, I watched from beneath my leaves as the men in red slaughtered everyone I knew. I lay very still beneath my autumn coverings. Even when the iron blade came plunging down into the leaves and slicing the skin on my leg. I did not move.

I was a child. The only child of the tree people. I alone live on. Surrounded only by the trees that, along with the birds and the rabbits, became my only friends. No one ever knew of my existence.

THE RIDGE

I am a writer.

Until tonight, I had forgotten that. Not really forgotten, just had pushed it to the back burner. I had lost faith in my abilities and myself. I didn't really understand why, until tonight. Then it hit me with crystal clarity. I had a shoulder critic, which I couldn't deal with.

Every writer has a critic that sits upon his shoulder telling him all sorts of things.

"Is that the best you can do?"

"Do you really think anyone wants to read this crap?"

"Why don't you quit hiding behind this computer and get a real job? You're for sure not accomplishing anything here."

"If you really think your stories are good, you are deluding yourself."

That type of thing. After a while you learn to ignore that little bastard, at least until you finish your first draft.

Now I must be really dense because until tonight I didn't realize that I had two of those little goblins to contend with. It wasn't just my own self-doubt sitting on my shoulder; I had a bigger critic looking over it. He was saying the same damn things. He had been saying it all along, but I just didn't hear him. Until late this afternoon. I had fired up the word-processor and had just typed a title, when he walked in.

"The Ridge." Says he. "What's it about?"

"Don't know yet." I answer. "Just thought it sounded good."

In case you're wondering, the Ridge is where he gets his beer and I get my wine. We live in a dry county and a trip to the ridge is an event.

"I could write that story." He says.

"Nope, it's mine." I reply. "Besides, I thought of it first."

"Well, I'll use your pen name, how's that?" He asks.

I answer, getting a bit indignant, "That's ok, I'll write it myself."

"I can write it better." He says.

"I'm not so sure of that." I reply. My ego was really getting bruised here.

Then his eyebrows went up. He didn't have to say a word. All of a sudden I knew why my writing had been terrible for the last year. Why I had lost my enthusiasm and drive. It was because of him. Why, oh why, hadn't I seen it before?

Maybe it was because to the outside world, he bragged on me. His wife, the writer. Maybe because when he knew I was down, he would say something like, "Honey, why don't you go work on a story and get your mind off things?

"Maybe, maybe, maybe.

Right after this conversation, he decided we needed to go to the ridge. He was out of beer. He was drinking my wine. Maybe that's why he was so obnoxious. So we went.

All the way there, what he had said irked me. I thought about other little things he had said in the past.

"Honey, are you sure you want to word it just that way. I would have phrased it..."

"Sweetheart, don't you think that sentence needs a little more explaining?"

"Dear, you have the education and the vocabulary. Why don't you use it?"

Little put-downs. Tiny ones. Barely noticeable. Yet, because of them, I was losing my voice. The more I thought about it, the madder I got. By the time we got home two hours later, my blood was boiling. I didn't know what to do about it.

You've got to realize here, that I'm really a timid person. I hate confrontations. If I opened my mouth, I knew we were going to fight. I said nothing. Just went about my business of cooking dinner.

While my loving other half and my children were stuffing their mouths with tacos, I was contemplating my options as I ate my burrito.

An old battered pickup truck pulled into the driveway and interrupted my wonderfully monstrous thoughts. Turned out it was one of the raggedy mountain men. My spouse had pulled him out of a ditch, one dark rainy night last week.

Everyone here on the mountain knows that my man was into guns. Powerful guns. This guy was no different. He had one to sell. Nothing spectacular, just an SKS carbine. Normally my other half would have passed on it. We already had two. This guy was so pitiful, with his sad story to tell that he took pity on him and bought it. That's when the light bulb went off in my head.

I knew, just knew that my darling would want to go out and shoot it. I was right. It wasn't an hour later before he said, "Think I'll go try it out."

"Hey, if wait until I get the kids to sleep, I'll come with you." I said, making sure the kids weren't around to hear me.

Sounds good." He replied.

Three hours later, we were on the road. He wanted to go to our favorite shooting place, about four miles away. On the way to the ridge. To the end of a little dirt road. If you didn't stop at the end of the road, you would go over the side of the mountain. About three hundred feet. Straight down.

Flashlights in hand, we walked out to the stand of rock that perched precariously on the ledge. My darling shot off twenty-six of the twenty-seven rounds he had loaded into the thirty round magazine.

"Want to shoot off the last one, hun?" He asked.

"Sure." I replied. I took the gun, aimed and fired.

Tomorrow morning, I suppose I'll call the police. Report him missing. I'll them everything. Almost. I'll tell them about how much he had been drinking yesterday. The guy at the liquor store will back me up on that one. So will the old farmer, down the road, whom we stopped and talked to on the way back. In fact, all the neighbors will talk about how crazy he was when he was drinking.

"What about when he was sober?" The police will ask.

"Never saw him without a beer in his hand." Most of them will reply.

I'll tell the police about the SKS and the guy he bought it from. I'll let the kids tell the police how he loved to shoot his guns. How every time, he got a new one; he took it out to shoot.

I won't tell them I went with him. I won't tell them I managed to drop my lighter in the floorboard every time we passed a neighbor's house. I won't tell them where we went. I won't tell them it took me almost four hours to walk home. I won't tell them I hid any gun, the ones that are my personal favorites. They can take the rest of them away, if they wish. I have no need for them.

Tonight, I won't think about what I have done.

Tonight, I am writing alone.

Tonight, I am a writer.

VANITIES

Clark Danner gazed through the open dressing room door at his wife, Elise, sitting at her make-up table. He could see her reflection in the mirror above and once again realized how honored he was to have her for his wife. Elise was beautiful. A former fashion model and twenty years younger than Clark, she made him the envy of his colleagues. Many of the other women considered her shallow because of her so-called vanity, but Clark knew that she was only attempting to preserve her beauty for him. She had told him so, many, many times.

Tonight as he watched her apply the creams and lotions to her skin, he could tell she was deeply troubled about something she was seeing in the mirror. Yet, he did not want to interrupt her at her regimen. He knew she would be finished in a few moments.

Instead, he thought about the new cream he was researching at the lab. It had already passed Draise testing and now had only to pass human tests to be FDA approved. Another year, maybe two, then Merclyn Laboratories could market the miracle cream of the century. Guaranteed to begin to vanquish wrinkles with the first use. Overnight, the user would see visible results. Depending on the depth of the lines, flawless skin could be promised within two weeks to a month. After that, once a week coverage for maintenance would keep the demand for the product going. It promised to be a boon for the company, a product to lift the threat of impending bankruptcy. If

Merclyn Cosmetics could hold on for one more year, the market price for stock would sky-rocket. Then the company and its employees would have job security for years to come.

Clark turned his attention back to Elise, watching as she frowned at her reflection in the mirror. Rising, he walked to the door of the dressing room.

"What's troubling you, dear? I hate it when you frown. Have I done something to make you unhappy?" he asked.

"No, it's not you. It's me, I mean, my face. Look at it. I'm getting crows-feet. No matter what I do, they're there. Damn, I'm only twenty-five. It is just not fair." she replied.

"Hon, I don't mean to sound condescending, but they aren't even noticeable. I'm sure no one has seen them but you." he said.

"That doesn't matter. Just the fact that I know is enough."

"Listen to you," he said, trying to tone down the impatience in his voice, "surely you are not going to let something that minor upset you."

"Look, you're the hot shot researcher for Merclyn. If you really loved me, you would help me. There's got to be some way to stop this, before I go all wrinkles and you stop being proud of me." she said, her expression turning into a pout.

"Darling, I'm sorry. I didn't realize how much it meant to you. Now, don't look so unhappy. I did not mean to upset you so. Do you forgive me?" he asked.

When she raised her face to his, her eyes were brimming with tears.

"I forgive you. But promise me, you'll try to find something that will help. Please?"

"Sweetheart, I probably shouldn't be telling you this, but we are working on something. The testing so far shows it has amazing results. As soon as we complete the volunteer testing and it has government approval, I'll bring it home for you. Is it a deal?" he asked.

"What kind of results, Clark? Tell me everything." Elise said excitedly.

As Clark filled her in on the details of the animal tests and the hopes for the product, he could see her eyes shine with anticipation.

"But how long will it take you to get it approved? It sounds like it will be years away. I want it now, Clark. Let me be one of your volunteers. Please, Clark? You could really check the results with me. You're here with me every night and you could see. Please, Clark?"

Her begging, he knew, would break him. She knew full well that he could deny her nothing. At that moment he regretted telling her anything at all about the cream.

She rose from her seat, putting her arms around his neck, "Please?" she asked, once again.

"Okay, as long as you promise to follow my instructions. I'll smuggle out a small jar tomorrow." he said.

Clark's mind was reeling. He knew what he was doing was unethical. But if it worked for Elise, then half the battle was over. With her, and the testing done at the Los Angeles lab, he could pad the results slightly. Possibly getting the product on the market ahead of schedule. Besides, Elise was pacified now. He knew she would repay him in bed tonight.

"Let's go to bed, Elise." was all he needed to say.

* * *

At four-thirty, before he left his lab, Clark rummaged the cabinets for a proper size jar. He could still hear Elise's voice ringing in his ears from this morning.

"You won't forget the cream, will you Clark? I can't wait to try it."

As everyone had already left for the day, Clark was sure he would not be seen removing the cream. His conscience had been bothering him all day, yet he had promised Elise. To break a promise to her, meant the risk of losing her. Finding a jar and filling it, he placed it in his briefcase and left the lab, locking the door behind him.

Knowing that he would see Elise happy and smiling when he returned home, made the drive in rush hour traffic bearable. Clark stopped at a neighborhood drugstore and bought a box and wrapping paper. He wanted this to be his finest gift to her, ever. He sat in his car and wrapped his present, thinking once again how lucky he was to have her.

Once he had the package to his satisfaction, he started the Volvo and drove the rest of the way home.

Elise met him at the front door, a happy smile on her face.

"Did you bring it, Clark?" she asked, her excitement   almost childlike, "I can't wait to try it. But later, after dinner. I even fixed you something special. Just for being so sweet."

"Then over dinner, I will give it to you. But right now, let me get out of this suit." he said.

While he was changing, Elise could hardly conceal her impatience. She asked one question after another about the cream. He could tell her biggest concern was if it would really work. After repeatedly assuring her, she hooked her arm through his and led him to the dining room. He was surprised to see not only candles, but also an ice bucket of champagne sitting by his chair.

"I told you it was a special dinner," she whispered in his ear, "but afterward, dessert will be even better. Now, pour us some bubbly darling, while I bring in dinner."

When the meal was over, Elise began clearing the table. Clark took the chance to retrieve the box from his briefcase. He had just placed it on the table in front of her chair, when she emerged back into the room. Her attention was immediately drawn to the brightly covered package.

"Is this it, Clark?" she asked, ripping the paper into shreds.

"That's it." he said, raising his glass. "A toast: to the end of crows-feet. In fact, to the end of wrinkles forever."

"That, I will drink to." Elise replied.

Two hours later, he was spent from the thank you Elise had given him in bed.

"I'm going to take a shower. Then go down and watch some TV, while you do your thing. That be all right?" he asked.

"That's fine, sweetheart. I can't wait any longer to try this stuff. I'll come down and join you when I'm done." she said.

"Just remember to follow the instructions I gave you. You should be pleasantly surprised in the morning." he said, swinging his feet to the floor and heading for the bath.

* * *

The next morning, Clark bent and kissed his wife's neck as he sat before her mirror.

"Well, do you see any difference?" he asked.

"No, I don't think so. I don't know. I'm not sure. Maybe." she answered, then continued, "You know, I had the strangest dream last night. I saw a face at the window and the longer I looked, I realized it was me. Only I had even deeper crows-feet then I do now. It was so scary, I woke up shaking."

"It was probably just your sub-conscious telling you that you are making too much out of nothing. I wouldn't worry about it. After all, it was just a dream, right?"

"You're right, darling, just a dream." she replied.

* * *

Several days passed and Elise said nothing more about the dream. Every morning, Clark told her she was looking better than the day before. That seemed to calm the jitters, he felt she was experiencing. He figured she finally realized she was using an experimental drug and deep down she was scared. But it was working, her tiny crows-feet were all but invisible.

On the fourth morning, Elise was visibly upset as she came into the dressing room.

"Clark, I had that dream again last night." she said, standing in the doorway. "Hell, I've had it every night since I began using this stuff. But, last night was the worst. The face in the window was old; absolutely haggard. And Clark, it was me!"

At that, Elise sat and put her face in her hands, sobbing hysterically.

"Elise, darling. Look in the mirror. Your face is flawless. Like porcelain. Come on now, look."

Calming somewhat, she shook her head no.

"Give me a few minutes. I'm sure my eyes are all red and puffy now." she said.

"O.K. Take your time, sweetheart. Right now, I've got to head for the lab. I'll tell you what. Why don't you meet me at the office and we'll go out for dinner? I want to show off the most beautiful woman in the world."

Putting her arms around his waist, she looked up and said, "You always know just the right words to say."

"And about the dreams, if you have another one tonight, just quit using the stuff. I think we have reached the point where it would be best to just do weekly maintenance. Then you won't be thinking about it so much. Now, I've got to run. I'll see you about four-thirty, right?"

At dinner, Elise appeared more like her old self. After eating and dancing, they arrived home late. While Clark assured himself that the house was locked tight, Elise removed her make-up and applied her cream. In bed, she cuddled close as they fell asleep. Two hours later, Clark was awakened by her screams.

"Another dream, darling?" he asked softly.

"Oh, Clark, it was horrible. My face was nothing but a skull." she answered between sobbing breaths.

"Okay. That's it, no more cream. It is just possible you might be reacting to some ingredient. That might be causing your nightmares. Tomorrow, I'll check with the lab in L.A. and see what's happening there. All right, hon? It's over. I promise, no more dreams."

Slowly, he coaxed her still shaking body back down beside his. He was feeling guilty for telling her about the cream at all. He should have waited until it had been approved. It was killing him to see her so unhappy. And yet, her face was flawless; absolutely perfect. He allowed that thought to lull him back to sleep.

The alarm rang and as Clark fumbled to hit the off button, he turned to look at his sleeping wife. His own scream, rising in his throat brought him to total wakefulness. Beside him in the bed was the body of his wife. Only somehow, some way, she had aged beyond comprehension. It was when he realized that his scream had not woken her, that he knew she must be dead.

WISHFUL THINKING

She sat at the window, contemplating the clouds as they wisped across the full moon. Mae Adams spoke silently to the heavens. With as much power as she could muster, she begged the universe for her salvation. Mae prayed to the unknown for deliverance from her life, as she knew it. If there were truly alien beings in the cosmos, and they were truly taking humans from the planet earth, she implored them to come rescue her. Only away from everything that she knew, did she feel she would find happiness and respite.

Mae had already considered suicide, allowing her spirit to join those of the afterlife. To her catholic mind, that meant going to hell. Do not pass go, do not collect two hundred dollars. Her life was miserable, true, but she had no desire to enter into the realm of the eternally damned.

During the past six months, she had placed herself in situations where she had been positive she would be killed. Although, she wasn't sure of the interpretation of her actions. When she would do these things, such as deliberately driving into the mists of the recent Los Angeles riots, she questioned if her priest would accept her death as an accident or intentional suicide. In the end, it hadn't mattered. She was still alive.

In her mind she had only one option left to escape the world she felt had been so callous and savage. Tonight, like every night, she sat in her window-seat holding her crystal. Watching for a sign that would confirm that whatever life existed beyond the stars had heard her heartfelt pleas.

She had embraced New Age philosophies, despite her severe religious upbringing, months before. Her conviction was strong that her crystals somehow linked her telepathically with the supreme power of the universe. It was the basis behind her intense cries to the unknown. She consistently affirmed, in her thoughts, that one-day they would come.

Most nights, she would fall asleep with her head resting against the cool panes of glass. Tonight was different. Tonight she felt nervous, jittery. Tonight, she could feel a humming deep within the quartz crystal she now gripped tightly in her left fist. Tonight was different. She could feel it. Her heart was singing.

Mae could sense the alien craft before she actually saw it. The skin prickled on the back of her neck as she felt the tension build within her. Her eyes scanned the darkened sky. She blinked, quickly as not to miss whatever was there.

Bordering on hyperventilation, she had to close her eyes in an effort to control her breathing. Opening her eyes, moments later, she saw it. It took her breath away to gaze upon the craft. Circular in shape, it appeared seamless and without windows or decorations, excepting the rows of multi-colored lights forming an immense triangle on the underside. The ship was large --totally overshadowing the neighbor's yard and street as it hovered several hundred yards above her back lawn. Her hands immediately clutched her chest as she uttered an audible gasp.

She watched in both fear and fascination as a beam of blue light began a downward path from the ship. Within seconds, she was bathed in the cool light. As she looked around and saw herself rising. She glanced back, toward the now empty room, saying what she hoped would be a final goodbye, as the light drew her into the vessel.

The light blinked out and she found herself standing alone in solid white emptiness. Her eyes darted in all directions. She supposed it was a room, yet she could not see a door or even a corner. She fought back the rising panic, swallowing repeatedly as she held back the scream she felt forming in her throat.

"Relax. Be calm." A quiet voice filled the room. "You are safe now. Your voice has been heard. We have come in answer to your call."

Mae could hold on no longer. The scream escaped her lips just before her eyes rolled into her head and she fainted to the floor.

Mae opened her eyes slowly. Looking around, she saw that she was in a different room. It still had no doors or corners that she could see, but the walls were painted a pale green. A light was glowing from a source she could not locate. She felt beneath her and found she was lying on a platform, a bed she supposed, made of soft ticking covered with a thin silver blanket.

She looked down at her body, and was almost surprised to find that she was still wearing the same frumpy housecoat and worn out slippers.

A shadow in movement caught her eye. Slowly, she turned her head in its direction. She almost giggled in delight at the little form that stood less than five feet away.

"This is perfect." she thought.

"Perfect? How so, is it perfect?" The small gray creature asked.

Mae could only stare at the being. He had read her mind. More amazing was that he, or it, was exactly like what she had read about in countless books and articles on alien contact.

He stood about four feet high, so thin that he appeared fragile. His head, reminding her of a group of mentally handicapped children she had seen as a child, was much too large for its body. He was gray all over, and try as she might, Mae could not see any lip, ears or body hair of any kind. His eyes fascinated her -- large, tear-shaped and black, they slanted upward at perfect angles to each other. His arms seemed insect-like while his hands had the appearance of claws. "Why, he is identical to the pictures in Whitley Strieber's books." she thought.

"I am sorry. Did I offend?" the alien asked.

Still flabbergasted, she finally found her voice.

"Well...no. Just surprised me a bit, that's all." She replied.

"We do not wish to frighten or harm you in any way. My name is Zot. I am here to provide you with any needs you may have."

"Thank you, Zot. I just can't believe that this is really happening to me. I expect to wake up any moment and find it was only a dream." She didn't add that was what had happened so many times before.

"No. Those were not dreams. We were just preparing you. We had to be sure that this was what you wanted."

"So, I have been here before." She exclaimed. "How far are we from the earth now?" she asked.

"We are cruising in front of your moon. Come, I will show you." He said, walking to what she saw now was a flat wall. Almost instantly a porthole appeared and Mae was looking down at earth.

"How did you do that?" She asked, "I mean, I didn't see you push any buttons."

"To coin an Earth expression, here you create your own reality. You wish to see out, you think it, and it is there. You are in need of nourishment, you think it and it will appear. It is the same principal for all things aboard this ship." He answered.

Looking back at the earth, Mae asked the question that intrigued her most.

"Where will we go from here?"

"We have stayed close to your planet only long enough for you to make your decision. If you wish to stay with us, we will take you to many worlds and you will see many things. Should your choice be to return to your planet, you must tell us now. We will not be returning here for many years to come." Zot replied.

"I have no desire to return, Zot. There is nothing there for me except loneliness and boredom. I wish to see the worlds you have spoken of."

"Then it is settled. I will inform the others." Walking to the opposite wall, he paused momentarily as a door appeared. It opened and he was gone.

"This is truly happening." Mae said aloud. Her joy was almost childlike as she kicked off her ratty slippers and twirled around the room.

Looking again out the porthole, she saw that they were pulling away from the moon. In fascination, she watched the earth and its satellite quickly become tiny specks among the stars. Her mind was spinning as they first passed Mars and then the giant gas planet, Saturn.

Overwhelmed, she thought of a chair to sit down. Within seconds, one appeared. Amused, she said, "No, too hard. I want a soft, easy chair." As quickly as the first had appeared, a plush beige recliner replaced it. Mae lowered her body into it and allowed her exhaustion to take over. She was soon asleep.

When Mae awoke, she saw that the lights in the room had been dimmed, yet the room was not totally dark, just bathed in shadows and the porthole had been closed. Mentally, she said "Window". The porthole reopened and she saw the heavens pass around her. For as far as she could see, she was surrounded by stars. Some bright, some dim yet the only the twinkling broken the blackness beyond the window.

Mae wished that Zot would come back. She had so many questions to ask. She wondered if she would ever get all the answers. A rumbling deep within her reminded her that she had not eaten for a while. She wasn't sure how long she had slept, but from the intensity of her growls, she knew it had been several hours.

"Table and chair." she said.

"I wonder," she repeated quietly, "Steak and Lobster."

Instantly the requested food items appeared before her on the table.

"A glass of white wine and a baked potato with butter." she said. Those items also appeared.

"Yes, I'm going to like it here." she thought as she took her first bite of the lobster.

—

MISS AMY'S GHOST

On the morning of February 8, 1862, Amy Foster killed her husband. She turned white - dead white - when she realized what she had done. I found myself in the middle of a moral dilemma. Should I help the lady who had been so good to me? Or, should I turn her over to the law, so justice (such as it was in those days and times) could be served. I chose the former option.

Within moments, Mrs. Foster had composed herself.

"What should I do, Colleen?" she had asked, still holding the bloody kitchen knife in her hand.

"Well, Ma'am, it seems we should get rid of the body before Cook gets back. Won't do if the others find out."

Mrs. Foster looked at me and smiled.

"And, how do you suggest, we do that?"

I thought about it for just a minute and then had an idea.

"Well, Ma'am, Foreman had the boys digging a new well and it must be ready because I saw Jacob putting a cover on the old one early this morning."

I started rushing my words, "Foreman says that the old one is full of sulfur and stinks to high heaven. If'n we can get the body in there, no one would notice the smell. At least that's my way of thinking."

Which is exactly what we did. No one saw us, and by the time Cook returned from the village, it was a done deal. You couldn't even tell there had been a killing in the kitchen.

I guess I should explain why I was so willing to help Mrs. Foster. The answer is simple; she was a good woman. A good woman tied down to a cruel and hateful man twice her age. I wasn't sorry at all she had killed the man, it meant that he could no longer slip into my room at night and force his favors on me. I was her indentured servant, her parents had given her my contract four years earlier as a wedding present. The hope that this might win me my freedom played a part in it also. It didn't work out that way, no sir, not that way at all.

Miss Amy, as I started calling her, was real strong those first few days after her husband disappeared. She played her role perfectly. When, come to find out, the village harlot had moved on, some folks even hinted that old Mister Foster had gone with her. Other folks suspected he was dead somewhere, killed by a damn Yankee but they never did find his body. After a year, Miss Amy stopped wearing her widow weeds and started stepping out in society. That was when it really all began. That was the night she began going crazy.

She was happy that night. There was a ball in Savannah, and nothing was going to stop her from attending. For weeks, I measured and sewed until I got her new gown just the way she wanted it. The color was a perfect sky blue, matching her eyes exactly; the taffeta material shimmered and rustled as she twirled around. She was so excited and I was excited for her. I guess it was the excitement that gave me the courage to ask how much longer my indenture contract was for.

"For life, Colleen. For life."

My jaw must have hung in disbelief, so she went on, "You don't really think I could let you go now, do you? Knowing what you know?"

She just stood there and stared at me. There wasn't any hatred or anger in her eyes, just this faraway look that baffled me at the moment.

"Besides where could you go? You belong here with me, Colleen. I need you."

That said, she swept down the staircase and out to the coach that was waiting. I thought about her words a lot that night and came to the understanding that she was right. I had nowhere else to go. Miss Amy was good to me; after all she had just given me all those black clothes from her mourning period. With a bit of lace and a few frills, they could be made up into something pretty. And she didn't treat me like a servant much anymore either. More like a poor relation. In the end I decided I didn't have it so bad, after all.

She got home from the ball early that night, looking like she had seen a haint or something. As I helped her undress, I asked.

"There was a man there tonight that looked enough like James to be his twin. He was just standing there, in a corner, by himself. When I asked about him, no one could recall ever seeing him. In fact, they said there were no men there that looked like James. Made me feel like I was going out of my mind."

"You mean no one else saw him?" I was sure my eyes were wide.

"No one. I am sure he was there, I am sure of it."

"I'm sure he was ma'am. You're not the sort to be seeing things." I said, hoping to reassure her and myself also.

It wasn't long before she started seeing him everywhere. On the grounds, in the village, at others houses. Only problem was, no one else saw him. The rumors then, first in the slave quarters spreading quickly to the entire community. They said that she had killed him and his ghost had come back for his revenge.

Almost as quickly as society had accepted her back in, they began to shun her. No longer was she invited to the fancy balls and the quiet suppers. No men came to call, which was surprising due to all the money she had. She began to see this man in the house. Staring at her from darkened hallways or lurking in the shadows of a room. Most of the house servants were free persons and before much time passed the ones that could were gone. It was only me and the colored girl who had been Cook's helper. Yet we managed. The girl could cook a decent meal and I shut up the parts of the house that we were not using. Before the year was out, President Lincoln delivered his famous emancipation proclamation. Another year passed, the Great War

ended, and the slaves were freed. All of our slaves left
- even the girl.

That was when Miss Amy came up with the
idea of moving west. She had heard of a place called
San Francisco. A place she said, we could start over
and leave this wretched place behind. I was more than
happy to do that, the carpetbaggers were beginning to
flood the town and everything was either in short
supply or highly expensive. Yet I stood my ground
first.

"Miss Amy," I said, "I'll be most happy to go
with you to San Francisco. First, though, you have to
do something for me."

"What's that Colleen?"

"Give me my contract, so I can tear it up. The
slaves are free now, and I want to be."

Quietly and calmly, she walked over to James'
picture handing on the sitting room wall. Lifting it
from its hook, she threw the portrait into the
fireplace. Now exposed was the safe. Opening it, she
rummaged through the papers inside and eventually
extracted a single sheet.

"It's yours, Colleen. Do with it what you will."

Although I couldn't read, I did recognize my
name and my mark on the paper. I tore it into tiny
shreds and tossed them on top of the painting burning in
the fire.

"When do we leave?" I asked.

"As soon as I can make the arrangements." She stated emphatically.

She did that quickly. She sold the house and grounds to the sleaziest Yankee I had ever seen and had booked passage to Saint Louis. Within three weeks we were on our way. I had never seen a big city before and Saint Louis both excited and frightened me at the same time. Miss Amy loved the sights and sounds of the city. And the city loved her. For the first time in months, there was no talk of the man who looked like James.

We stayed in Saint Louis for three months, waiting for warmer weather to travel west. Miss Amy rented a house and became an overnight socialite of the city. She began introducing me as her sister.

"We have to teach you to talk proper English, Colleen." She said to me one evening. "After all, now you're family."

"Could you teach me to read and write?" I asked.

"Well, to be of good blood, you have to know how to do that. Don't worry your head none, by the time we get to San Francisco, I'll turn you into a proper lady."

I smiled and was happy. No longer was I Colleen O'Neal, indentured servant; she was introducing me as Colleen James, her sister. Her family was dead, so there was no one who could dispute any of the lies she told. We had fun in Saint Louis, yet by the time we left I was glad. She was beginning to get that haunted look in her eyes and I caught her more than once staring down the empty darkened hallways of the rented house. The madness was returning.

As we reached Kansas City, Miss Amy kept her promise. I could write my name and hers, knew the alphabet and could read simple sentences from the bible she carried. Santé Fe showed even more improvement; I could read and write almost as well as her and no longer spoke with what she called "Irish brogue". I was becoming a lady.

Amy, which is what I called her then, was slipping away faster. She saw James at every stop of the stagecoach. Other passengers were beginning to look upon me with pity because I had to take care of my sister. Our roles were reversing. Now I was the strong one who made the decisions. It got worse as we got further west.

In Tucson, she became hysterical, ranting and raving about James waiting at the coach for her. In our hotel she refused to leave the bed, because James was sitting in the chair opposite her. Of course, he wasn't there, but you couldn't convince her. We missed the stage and were forced to stay in Tucson another two weeks. It was then I came up with another plan.

Everyone at the hotel knew she was crazy. Her screaming kept other guests awake at night and her daytime ramblings caused others to look at her with raised eyebrows. She refused to eat saying that death was better than living with James watching her. Now she was insisting that he was sitting in the chair holding the same kitchen knife as she had used on him. Nothing I said would convince her. I had about a week before the stage was due and there was no way I was going on to San Francisco with her.

The decision made, I made my way to the kitchens of the hotel using the excuse that she wouldn't even drink tea unless she knew I had made it myself. While in the kitchen, I pocketed the vial of arsenic kept there for the mice. I myself began poisoning her tea.

Five days later, Colleen James was dead. Amy Foster buried her sister in Tucson and then continued, grief-stricken, on to San Francisco. No one suspected the switch, as it was I who had checked into the hotel and I who had made the travel arrangements on to California. The hotel staff was very sympathetic and helped with the arrangements and the disposal of my sister's belongings.

I arrived in San Francisco and was greeted at the hotel by the owner. He informed me that the hotel had telegraphed my loss and to be expecting me. Later I purchased a large house in the city and hired a few servants. I, Colleen O'Neal former indentured servant, now lived in the lap of luxury. I was invited into society. I had male callers. I had it all. Everything Amy Foster once possessed was now mine, along with her name.

Including James. He sits in the chairs of my house or stands in the hallways. Watching me. He is real, I know he is. Amy stands beside him, never saying a word. Just waiting. As if they know, it's only a matter of time before I break.

THE CHURCH ON THE HILL

The town wasn't that old. A little more than a hundred years had gone by since it had been settled. Nor was it pretty or quaint. Actually quite ugly and dirty. However it was a good Baptist town. A town where membership to the big church on the hill was almost mandatory. It was a town where many secrets were hidden behind closed doors. A town where no one spoke of its' origins or the original settlers. Only four remained that remembered the turn of the century farmhouse which oversaw the town; where the church now stood. Stella Dixson was one of those four.

Stella thought she would go to her grave with that secret. She was one of four in the town of three thousand that did not belong to the big Baptist church. One of remaining four who were shunned. One of four who were routinely tormented not only by the children of the town but also their parents. The other three were elderly like her and lived near the outskirts. They escaped much of the abuse by refusing to come into town. Stella lived on the hill, across the street from the big church. For her, there was no escape. She was seventy-two, far too old to move, far too stubborn to give in.

This was her town. She had been born and raised here. She had married here. She had lived in this house for all of her seventy-two years. What did she care that her yard was papered at least once a week? Or that the paint on the outside was dingy, cracked and peeling from all the years of rotten eggs thrown at its' sides? Or that the children called her a witch and the parents called her worse when she made her weekly walk to the town store for groceries? None of that mattered to her. She was a thorn in the side for the whole town. Of that, she was rather proud.

Stella watched with interest as the realtor showed the empty house next door. Many of the young couples would look over at her house and yard, then at the agents who would whisper to them. They would shake their heads no and get in their cars and leave. The house had been on the market for over a year and although Stella knew the asking price was low no one had made an offer for it. Until last month.

Stella had seen the young couple arrive. They had stepped out of the car and looked at the house. They had looked at her house. The realtor arrived. For the first time in months, the realtor actually unlocked the front door and showed the inside. An hour passed. They emerged from the house. The young woman pointed at Stella's house. The realtor leaned forward and whispered. The woman looked at her husband and shrugged. They had moved in a week ago.

The townsfolk had tried to welcome them. They had been turned away at the front door. The Pastor had gone the day before to invite them to church. He never made it to the door. The young husband met him in the yard and after a moment of conversation, the Pastor was heading back across the street to his church. His face was grim.

Today was Halloween. Services were in full swing at the church. Stella was sure the Reverend was preaching the evil of the pagan holiday. Only because it was Sunday, would the town's youth not come and destroy more of her house and yard. They would be in church.

The young couple was at home. Stella had just finished frosting a chocolate cake. Putting it in a cake keeper, she carried it out the door, down the steps and across the yard. She knocked on her neighbor's door. The young woman answered.

"You're Charlotte's granddaughter. Welcome back to Stanton."

"How did you know?"

"Child, you are the spitting image of her. Imagine me forgetting the look of my best friend."

"You were my grandmother's best friend?"

Stella nodded her head. "Even though she was ten years older than me. I even use to baby sit your mother. She was such a pretty child, and it was so sad when she came down with tuberculosis and had to be hospitalized. In fact you almost bought her house. It's the next one down."

Within moments, Stella was ushered into the living room and introductions were made.

"What made you come back?"

"Mama died about six months ago. She was never really well. We found a newspaper article in my mother's things. About the big fire here in town. It was so sad, all those people dying. My grandmother was one of them, wasn't she?"

"Your mother never told you?"

"No, my mother never said anything really. Only that she was dead. The article aroused my curiosity. We came here to look. Then we saw this house for sale. I felt like it was waiting for us."

"Maybe it was child." Stella said, a smile coming over her face.

Stella let her eyes wander around the room. Her gaze fell upon a wall icon hanging over the mantle. A smile touched the corners of her lips and her eyes twinkled.

"Did you tell any of the others any of this?"

"No." Came the husbands Tom's reply. "None of their business."

"Wise choices."

"Are all the people in this town so nosy?" Lilith asked. "The ones that showed up were full of questions."

"Yes, they are all like that. I don't think they will bother you anymore though. Especially now that you let me in. They'll be watching you, but I don't reckon you'll find any more darkening your doorstep."

"Why? Have we done anything so wrong?"

"You've done two things that are unforgivable in this town. Letting me inside your front door was one, the other is probably worse."

"What would that be?"

"You're not over there." Stella replied, nodding toward the front of the house and the church.

"Tell us about the fire, Stella. You were here, you remember." Lilith said in an almost pleading tone. "All we know is that a party was going on, it was Halloween night, and everyone in attendance died. What's the real story?"

Stella leaned back against the overstuffed sofa and took a deep breath. 'Ok, so maybe it's not going to my grave with me." She thought to herself. Taking a few more deep breaths, she began, "Best to start at the beginning I suppose. Nine Scot and Irish families founded this town in 1899. They came here, which was then in the middle of nowhere, to live life their way. Without the hassles, as you young folk would say today. They named the town Harmony. For the first fifty years, everything went well. The families prospered and grew, new people moved into the community. Then a lone man came to town.

"He was an itinerant preacher. An evangelist, a man who could preach fire and brimstone till the Christian devil would shake in fear. He sat up a tent and began preaching. No one showed up. What he had not realized was this town believed and kept the old ways of our heritage. Other than believing all gods were one, we didn't much believe in the God of the Bible. That got him riled up. He would stand in his tent, night after night, condemning us to hell through a bullhorn.

Halloween came. I had just lost a baby. There was a gathering planed at the house that used to stand on that hill over yonder. I was too weak to go, but I talked my husband into going for the both of us. Told him he could come back and show me the party through his eyes. That was the last time I saw him, any of them."

Stella paused; a tear ran down her cheek. She lifted a coffee cup to her lips and took a small sip.

"Sometime after he left, I awoke. It was bright, as day, but the light was funny. It flickered. I crawled out of bed and went to the front window. The house was in flames. I ran across the street, but couldn't get anywhere close to the house. All the while I heard the preacher on the bullhorn declaring God's judgment on us. I'll never forget his words; "The fires of hell are consuming the evil of this place.

The next day the six people who had not attended the gathering, came together to sift through the ruins. We tried to find a reason. All we found was the remains of one door. It had been boarded over the handle, so it could not be opened. We knew then that the fire had been deliberately set and those inside had been meant to die."

"Oh, Stella, how horrible that must have been for you." Tom said quietly. His wife, still sitting on the arm of the recliner had tears running down her cheeks.

"So that is how my grandmother died. No wonder my mother never spoke of it. I cannot imagine how painful that was for you, for her, for all those who survived."

"How many of the six are still alive?" Tom asked.

"There are only four left." Stella replied.

"Call them Stella. Have them meet us here tonight. It's Samhain, Halloween. Let's give our ancestors and family a real goodbye." The young man said looking over the mantle.

"Will they come, Stella?" Lilith asked.

"I will persuade them." Stella responded with a smile. "I'm sure they will be glad of a gathering in Harmony again. After the preacher began moving his friends into the dead's homes. That's when they started calling the town Stanton. After him. That's his son sermonizing over there now."

At Seven PM that Sunday night, after the church on the hill was full to brimming. The four elderly members of Harmony gathered in the young couple's home. After introductions, Tom asked if they would like to begin. Everyone nodded their affirmation.

Lilith walked to the fireplace, pulled the icon from the wall over the mantle, and sat it in the center of the living room floor. They all joined hands in a circle around the pentacle. They began offering their prayers and farewells to the dead. Stella had made lists of everyone who had died in the fire. Each death was acknowledged and wished well in their new life. The ceremony went on for hours.

No one in the room noticed the sky outside. No one in the room noticed the flickering lights. Only when all the names had been read, all the blessings sent forth, did Stella notice the red lights. Breaking the circle, she went to the window.

The church on the hill was engulfed in flames. Those gathered in the room grabbed their coats and went outside. A heavyset fire marshal from a neighboring town stopped them.

"What happened?" Lilith asked.

"It's the worst tragedy I've ever seen. Everyone in the church is dead. No one got out."

"Do you know what caused the fire?" Asked Tom.

"No. We haven't got a clue. Where were you folks at? Did none of you see or hear anything?" The fireman asked the suspicion sounding in his voice.

"No, sir, we didn't. We were watching "Gone With the Wind" on tape." Lilith said.

"I can't believe you didn't hear anything." Came his response.

"Look at how old we are young man. We nearly ran these young people out of their house, us having the television set up so loud." Stella said.

"It the damnedest thing I've ever seen. I don't know if we will ever know the cause."

"Maybe it was God's judgment." Stella said.

ANSWERED PRAYER

The stranger appeared in the doorway and a scream began forming in my throat. Who was this man, why was he here? The thought of an outsider being this close frightened me. Who had let him in?

For ten years, I remained locked away in this tiny apartment, careful to surround myself by only what I know. Who I know. How dare someone intrude on me? Yet he only stood, as if waiting for an acknowledgement, framed in the sunlight from the hallway window. A golden aura radiated from him and looking at him with my tired eyes made my entire body relax. I had nothing to fear. He was the one I waited for.

I turned my wheelchair to face him and smiled.

"You've finally come."

"Only if you are ready."

"I've been ready for years."

"You must be sure, Agnes."

"I want out of this miserable life. What has it got to give me? I've spent years confined to this chair. My only companions in this life, are the pills I swallow to take away the pain that wracks my body. My own children ignore me, my friends already dead and gone. I'm ready for heaven. I've prayed for you nightly."

"You have been heard." He stepped closer and I got a better look at the man.

"You're not what I expected."

"Ah, and that was?" he smiled then, only to me it seemed more of a leer, a smirk.

"More angelic looking, I suppose. Not so dark and scruffy." I studied the man in front of me. Scruffy was a good word; even his suit didn't fit correctly. I began to have doubts.

"Are you sure it is your job to get me?"

"I'm what you've been praying for."

"I can't believe God sent you."

"What do you mean, you can't believe?"

"God's messengers are angelic, holy, perfect. And you are far from that." The man was positively dark, his hair, his eyes; even his stance was threatening.

"Which god? There are many. I assure you I came from the god who heard your prayers."

"There is only one God! I don't know who you are. Get away from me!" I tried to back the wheelchair away, the wall of the tiny room prohibiting my retreat. He moved forward another step. Fear made my pulse race and my movements' jerky. I could not maneuver and even if I could there was nowhere to hide.

"No, Agnes. There are many gods. You never called upon one by name. So, naturally the one next in line had the responsibility of answering your prayer." He said, advancing. Now he appeared larger, more muscular.

"No! No! No! I won't go with you. I won't!"

"You have no choice Agnes. You have already struck your bargain. It is time to go." The distance between us shortened, the seams of his suit began ripping.

"You're from the Devil. That's who you are."

"The Devil, Satan, Lucifer, whatever you wish to call him. He is a god also. It was his turn and your soul belongs to him. You assured that when you took more of your pain pills than prescribed. You have been slowly killing yourself for years. Suicide is never rewarded by the god you say you believe in. You deliberately forced the hand of the one you know as your god."

His laughter filled the small room. Now he stood within a foot of me. No longer did he look like a man, but more a demon from hell. He loomed over me; his skin dark and scaly, wings hanging at his sides as if ready to take flight, his mouth sneering in wicked grin.

I closed my eyes, feeling the tears run down my cheeks, knowing this had to be a nightmare. He wasn't real, he couldn't be. I wouldn't allow it to be. God wouldn't allow it to be. I felt him take my hands and then, nothing else.

When next I opened my eyes I found myself among mists, my frail body tossed and bounced by unseen hands. The pain was excruciating as I felt bone after bone break, muscle upon muscle bruise and rip. I thought I had known pain and loneliness and now I understood I had known nothing.

Here, wherever this place was, in my own hell, no one would hear my screams. No one would ever stop the pain.

—

BIG BERTHA

Bertha Trowbridge stood behind the counter at Wiley's One Stop Truck Stop and surveyed the crowd. Most decent truckers kept right on going past the seedy hole in the wall to the next stop closer to the city.

Big Bertha smiled as she took a ten from a large burly man who from the smell of him, hadn't bathed in a month or more. Although she carried over 400 pounds on her five foot four frame, she was fastidiously clean. Her long blond hair shimmered, even in the dim lights of the diner. She often overheard comments that if she would just lose two thirds of her bulk, she would be stunning. Yet Big Bertha had two habits that would keep her from ever attempting to set that goal for herself. She loved to eat especially fried foods; meat sandwiches a mainstay of her diet. And she loved to drink; hard whiskey mixed with soda early on in the evenings progressing to straight shots before oblivion took her over. A typical evening meal, eaten around midnight, as that was when she would get home from work, consisted of three or four one pound burgers, French fries and a pie or cake for desert. Generally before passing out just before dawn, she will have finished at least a fifth of sour mash.

All day long at the diner, she would stuff her face with pastries and donuts, washing it down with soda between customers.

"Time to start closing down, Berth." Wiley shouted from the kitchen.

Looking up at the clock she saw it was already a quarter of eleven. Scanning the room once more, she settled on the man in the corner booth. She had been flirting with him and several others earlier, but knew she must now make a decision. She pulled his ticket from her apron and walked toward his table, pausing long enough to staple an extra sheet of paper to the bill.

The little man hung back waiting for the other departing customers to leave first. When he finally stood in front of the cash register, he asked, "A good time you say?"

"The best you'll ever remember." Bertha replied with a smile.

"So how do we work this out?"

"Drive your truck to the rest area on the other side of town." Bertha looked furtively toward the kitchen. "I don't want Wiley to know I'm doing this, it'd mean my job"

"You going to pick me up there?"

"You bet. I don't live far from the stop."

She gave him a description of her car and assured him she would be waiting at the end of the ramp.

"I'll take the back roads, it's faster." She said, her grin warming the features of her face. "I'll even have time to pick up a bottle or two. Name you poison."

Big Bertha arrived at the rest stop fifteen minutes later, a fifth of sour mash and one of gin on the seat beside her. She did not have to stop for it, only had taken it from her well-stocked truck. She pulled through the truck stop with her lights out and went to the end of the ramp, almost back on the highway. As she waited, she thought about how easy this was. The clientele that visited her diner never cared how big she was. For them, anyone offering sex was a moment to be taken. Within five minutes, through her rear view mirror, she saw the little man making his way down the ramp.

"You know, I don't even know your name." Bertha said when the man was in the car.

"Tony. Just Tony."

"Married?"

"No, I'm not married. Is this twenty questions or are we going to party?"

"Party it is." Bertha replied.

Turning the headlights on and putting the car in gear, she pulled onto the deserted highway. Not talking at all, she drove to the next exit and turned left. Two blocks later, they pulled into her driveway.

"You live here alone?" Tony asked.

"All of me, all by myself."

"But it's so big."

"Yep. But it's all mine. My granny left it to me."

Bertha smiled as she reached for the door handle. Most of the men she brought here had the same reaction when they saw the old antebellum house.

"Come on, I'll show you around. If you're interested."

It was the man's turn to grin. Inside, the house was just as it had been left to Bertha. The furniture a collage of heavy Victorian to late art deco.

"This way to the kitchen." She said. "I'll make us a drink."

"Got any vermouth?" A gin martini sounds good." He said, following her down the dimly lit hallways.

The kitchen was enormous, larger than the dining area Bertha worked in every day. She reached into the cupboard and brought out two glasses.

"Don't have a martini glass though, will a regular one work?"

"No problem." Tony said, his eyes busy taking in the room. A large commercial stovetop and oven filled one side and another wall was what appeared to be a walk-in refrigerator freezer. "You actually use all this stuff?" he asked.

"Why not?" Bertha replied. "My granny had it installed when she turned the place into a boarding house in the sixties. Seemed kinda foolish to tear it all out."

Tony only nodded. "Where's the bedroom?"

"Let me refill our glasses first."

"Why bother? Let's just take the bottles."

Bertha smiled. No pretenses with this one, she thought to herself, he takes his drinking seriously. Grabbing the two bottles by their necks, she said, "This way."

Entering the downstairs bedroom, Bertha was pleased that she had remembered to make the bed this morning. The large king size waterbed overwhelmed the room, leaving little place for anything else. A dresser with a large mirror was the only other piece of furniture in the room, but the open door on the other side revealed a large walk in closet with a built in chest of drawers.

Tony had already sat his glass on the bookcase headboard of the bed and was beginning to shed his clothing. Bertha followed suit, not once ashamed of her body. Judging by the hardness of his manhood pushing against his underwear, this one would go for anything. Tony climbed on top of the covers. Bertha lay beside him and began stroking his chest, slowly allowing her hand to ease southward. Eventually, she climbed on top of the man.

When they had both spent themselves, they sat up in the bed and filled their glasses. Tipping their glasses to each other, they toasted that the night was young.

"I don't know about you, but I've worked up an appetite." Bertha said. "Want a hamburger before round two?"

"Sounds good."

"Ok, stay there if you want. I'll go fix them for us."

By the time Bertha returned with the burgers, Tony had finished off more than half the bottle of gin. Bertha, herself, had been drinking shots in the kitchen while cooking. Neither was feeling any pain. After eating, Tony suggested they get back to what he had come here for. Bertha complied.

As Tony lay beneath the large woman, he felt as if she was getting heavier. He could feel the bed board under the waterbed hard beneath his back. His hard-on was softening, yet Bertha didn't seem to notice. She stretched out her bulk over the top of him. His face was lost in the flab surrounding her enormous breasts. He tried to move and found he couldn't. The weight was too heavy. He tried to scream, but found that his voice could not penetrate the fat. He tried to breathe, yet found no air.

Bertha awoke the next morning at ten. As she opened her eyes, she saw what had happened yet again. Slowly she crawled off the man who lay beneath her. Going to the shower, she scrubbed her body of what she felt like was filth. Once clean, she wrapped the unfortunate man in the sheet and pulled him from the bed and through the hallways. Reaching the kitchen, she opened the large walk-in freezer. Unceremoniously she placed his body beside the one already there.

"Won't have to go grocery shopping this week." She said to herself. Closing the freezer, she went to get ready for work.

—

THE TRUTH OF BECOMING

"It is all a lie, simply a romantic myth. How we came to be is more natural, more ordinary than those who write about us would have you believe. On an entertainment level, I suppose their version receives more mileage. Yet, it is still a lie.

"Do you want to know the truth? You do? Are you sure? Will it make you afraid to walk outside? Will it make you fear your animals, your pets? I do not know. I really do not care."

I stared at the old man sitting across from me. He was different from the rest of those here, yet I didn't know why. He did not seem to fear me, nor did he look at me with pity. Unafraid to meet my gaze; his watery blue eyes were wide open beneath the heavy lids surrounded by weathered wrinkles lining his face. They never once left my face.

"You think I am delusional, don't you doctor?"

"No, Mr. Thomas. I have not said that. I am not a doctor of psychiatry, I cannot be the judge of your sanity."

"The other doctors have. That is why they keep me restrained."

"If I promise to free the binds, Mr. Thomas, then will you tell me your story?"

"Do you think that is safe, Doctor? The others, every doctor, every nurse, even the orderlies, they are afraid of me." I said, nodding at the Mutt and Jeff pair against the far wall.

"I'll take my chances, John. I can call you John, can't I? I don't believe you are mad or delusional. My specialty is a specific disease of the blood. I believe that is what you suffer from. I have met others like you before." He smiled then. More lines formed around his cheeks and nicotine stains covered the edges of his lips. I knew he believed what he said and I believed him and felt a faint light of hope. I began to relax.

"Let me move about and I'll tell you what you want to know."

I watched as he turned to the orderlies and nodded. They did not move but remained rigid as if standing their ground, offering only questioning glances.

"Gentlemen, I will repeat my request. Please remove the restraints from Mr. Thomas."

"Are you sure you want to do that, Doctor? We were told we were never to let him loose." The largest of the goons asked.

"I do not care what you were told. Loose the restraints and wait outside."

The smaller orderly shrugged. As a team, they came closer to my bed. Working quickly, they undid the leather straps and made a speedy retreat for the door. I could hear their sighs of relief when the solid steel slammed and locked between them and me.

"There, do you feel better, John?"

"Yes." I answered, flexing the muscles in my arms and legs. They had been bound tightly to the bed for so many hours that I questioned my ability to move them at all.

"Now for your part of the deal, John. You said you would tell me what has happened to you."

"What do you want to know? You have the file, there, in your hands. I'm sure the others have detailed my condition and made their conclusions."

"I haven't heard it from you, John. I want to hear it in your words. I want to know how you became this way."

"Back in the days when I had a wife and children. A farm and a life. You want me to start there?"

"That sounds as good a place as any."

No one had asked me that yet. I had to think. It was hard to remember. I knew the IV attached to my forearm pumped unknown drugs into my system. That was why I could not remember it all. Piecing things together, maybe I could do this. I reached down and removed the IV from my arm, slinging it to the other side of the room. I began.

"Last winter was hard in the Ozark hills; the air dry, the ground frozen for weeks. Enough so, that we all hoped that the insect pest population would die back a bit for the coming spring. By the middle of April, we all knew that was not to be. The warm weather and abundance of rain created an insect explosion. Grasshoppers defoliated every green shoot that made it out of the ground. Hornworms ate the tomato plants long before they put forth their first flower. Aphids covered any plant that had managed to escape any other bug. Fleas and ticks thickly covered the skin and fur of our pets. People carried fly swatters everywhere they went. Sitting out on the front porch to enjoy the cooler evenings became a wishful thing, an impossible dream.

Everyone I knew was inundated with unwanted small crawling creatures. Nothing less than an infestation; it became a plague. The EPA had recently banned our best ally, the only poison that would really deter the tiny beasts. By full summer, it was impossible to walk outdoors without an attack of some insect or another. The ticks were the worst of the lot, both dog and seed ticks, they were everywhere; in the grass, on the dirt, even crawling on the sides of the houses. They covered the windows, trying to force their way into any crack they could find. Most folks had taken to stripping on their doorsteps and having spouses' check for the blood-sucking creatures before entering their homes. No one cared if their neighbor saw them naked. Several children died of Rocky Mountain Spotted Fever or Lyme Disease. Many of the adults contracted it also, yet because they were stronger, most lived through it.

"County officials were called and responded, as most bureaucrats are liable to, that there was nothing they could do. Their only advice, keep your pets and yourselves inside. For most of us, that was no option at all. We kept our children in, but the cows still needed tending, the fields harvested and the multitude of other farm chores refused to wait for winter. So the adults continued to go outside, and became more diligent."

"So why didn't you leave John? What kept you there?"

The old man asked. As I looked at him, he reminded me of pictures I had seen of Einstein in his later years.

"Ah, good question, Doctor. Why? Because I couldn't afford to leave. We had taken every dime we owned to buy that place. We were mortgaged to the hilt. And even with the creepy crawlies, we felt they were preferable to the two-legged snakes you find in the city. It wasn't what we wanted for our children, the city, I mean. It was a tradeoff--big city lawyer or small town attorney. The choice was simple."

"So how did you cope?"

"We used bug sprays with high concentrations of DEET. We used it liberally. The local super center could not keep enough in stock. For me, it was not enough. One tiny tick. We overlooked a miniscule seed tick. At first, I did not know where upon my body it lodged. As the days went by, I became weaker and weaker, and finally my wife found the little feaster in the folds beneath the foreskin of my penis. The doctor assured us, when we went to have it removed, it was not the fever or the disease. He had no explanation of what I was feeling; only that perhaps it was the heat. I wasted away slowly. I took to my bed and there I died.

"I awoke. I awoke ravenous. Hungry beyond anything I had ever felt before. My wife tried to feed me. She tried all of my favorite foods. I couldn't hold them down and only violently threw them up again. She would spend hours stroking my face in an attempt to soothe me. The scent of her skin drove my mind crazy. Her smell was ambrosia. I would look into her green eyes and remember all of the good times. The simple joy of being with her. I knew our lovemaking days were over, yet God how I wanted her. To taste her one last time. To feel her auburn hair caressing my skin. Losing control, I bit her arm. Tasting her blood, I knew what I craved. As I sucked, I could feel her life force mingling with mine. Now we would, in truth, become one as her blood nourished my ravished body. The shock in her eyes devastated me and was more than she could handle. She fainted. She never awoke.

"Satiated for the moment, I saw what I had done. Wiping my face with the bed sheets, I did my best to compose myself. I walked into the living room and told my children to go to the neighbors and call their grandparents to pick them up. "Hurry!" I screamed at them. They ran.

"Soon, my father was at my door. He saw what I had become. Crawling around on the floor, licking up the blood that had spilled from the family dog. He opened the door and I raged by him. They found me, days later, at the auction barn sucking the blood from the last of the horses."

I quieted then. That was all I could remember until I woke up here in this cell. No one had explained anything to me. In truth, this old man was the first person who had talked to me directly since I opened my eyes.

"Beyond that, I have no recollection. I'm sure it is all there." I said, pointing to the file in his lap. "Is that what you wanted to know, Doctor?"

"They shot you in that barn, John. Not once, but several times. You appeared dead; the police called for the coroner. He discovered your heart still beating, so they brought you here. Your bullet wounds have disappeared, with no scars. Tell me why, John? Tell me what you are."

We stared at each other. I thought he would understand, I had supposed him to be a modern day Van Helsing or something.

***

The drugs no longer have a hold on me and I can feel my strength returning. I am hungry. I see the vein in his temple pulsating. It is a beckoning call. I leap. I feast.

***

I look down at the doctor's mangled body, or what remained of it. I must learn not to be so savage. I feel no real remorse, only a melancholy sadness. Had I not been so hungry, I might have let him live. He could have taught me much. I hear footsteps outside the door. Someone is coming. I am ready.

***

The bodies I left in my escape are of no consequence; I cannot let that bother me. They did not understand the need, the hunger, the lust for the taste of blood.

I am free, walking towards the bright blood red globe of the rising full moon hovering at the end of a road. The thirst is satisfied for now. I have become one of the undead. I smile at that thought. Had I known that the bite of a small miniscule tick created the vampire, I would have become immortal years ago. After all, how many of the damned things have I pulled off over the years? I begin to laugh; soon the sound fills the still silence of the night.

I must find others like me, they're out there, the old doctor had confirmed that for me. Even without his affirmation, it does not matter. They exist. Why else would so many write about us? All fiction begins with a morsel of truth.

WAITING FOR WINTER

The yard had grown up quickly this spring. Not having anyone around to cut it for her, Emma Thorpe had tried to ignore it. In essence, she attempted to ignore anything beyond her own front door. Not since she had seen him waiting.

The chickens were dead and the dog was dying; yet, Emma could do nothing to help. Her mail hadn't been fetched from the box in weeks. The last time she had tried to cross the threshold to get it, he was there at the foot of the stairs waiting. He was there still.

Emma had been born and raised in this house. For her first eighteen years, her father had protected her from him. For the next sixty, her husband had filled the post. After his death, her son had come home to live and had kept her safe. Now he was dead too and she was all alone. At ninety, Emma was frail. Her body hunched with the feebleness of age. Her mind still sharp, yet full of fear. She waited to die.

She sat daily in the rocking chair in the living room in front of the picture window. She watched as cars passed on the newly paved road. No one stopped. No one remembered the old widow who lived here alone. Truth of the matter was, none of her contemporaries were still alive. Their children had long left the rural community in order to build a life for themselves in the cities. Emma knew that there was no one to save her. The carefully stocked pantry was now almost empty. The refrigerator and freezer had been barren for weeks.

The car sat in the driveway. Emma could still drive but could not get past the front door. His shadow was still at the bottom of the front steps. The back door of the house was impossible for her. The lawn had grown up so much there that to her it appeared to be a jungle that she knew she couldn't manage. So she ate a single miserly meal a day hoping to last until winter. He would leave then.

The months passed. Emma continued to sit at the front window when she had the energy to pull herself from her bed. The leaves on the trees in the yard were turning the vibrant shades of fall. The grasses in the yard had long been brown, parched by the heat of the summer. He remained at the foot of the stairs.

Winter came. The first snowfall laid a blanket of white on the front lawn of Emma's home. She still sat in the rocking chair.

The new pastor of the communities only church was the first to ask about the house. Like a forgotten sliver in their fingers, the parishioners began to talk about Emma. Finally, someone mentioned that they had not seen her all year. The young pastor suggested that a few of them go to visit.

They walked up the drive to her front door. They could see her sitting in the front window. Knocking, they received no answer. The young pastor tried the handle and found it unlocked. He opened the door, immediately turning around to retch out the contents of the afternoon's potluck. They found her, sitting in her rocker dead. Her decayed body beginning to fall from her bones.

The young pastor went to his car to get his cell phone to call the sheriff, tripping at the bottom of the stairs. Looking down, he saw the remains of a large black snake. It's been dead longer than she has, he thought to himself as he made his way to his car.

—

LOST SOULS

The man stood motionless at the large picture window overlooking the street below. It was a perfect Friday night. A pregnant and heavy full October blood moon loomed over the horizon rising into a brilliant starlit sky. A thin smile was on his lips as he thought of how everything was in place: the moon, the stars, the day. It was All Hallows Eve, the high holy day of the dead. Patiently waiting, he watched the road. Occasionally he saw a child, costumed in the latest cartoon character craze or possibly a more traditional ghost, witch or vampire, run from house to house, candy bag open, expectation of special treats shown in their squeals of delight.

For Amos Mallory, it was indeed a special Halloween night. One of promise, one of expectation, one of special desires coming to fruition. For Amos, this Halloween was the one that his late wife would return to him. To sit in the leather chair beside the fire, share a brandy and conversation. It had taken him ten years to figure out how, but now there was nothing left to do but the ritual itself.

The candles were in place, the pentacle drawn upon the floor and Laura's body placed within the center of the five-pointed star. Amos looked down upon his wife. She was as beautiful as the day she had died. The fact that her body had been stolen from the morgue was now a distant memory and unsolved mystery in the minds of the community of High Gap. The freezer he had purchased to preserve her beauty had never let him down, The gentle hum soothing him in the basement corner while he researched and learned the secrets of reanimating his beloved.

Now, he was confident he was ready. All was prepared. He only needed one soul to exchange for the soul of his dear Laura and she would again be at his side. He would not have to wait long now. Young Timothy Bryan would be knocking on his door, to again torment him and expect a treat. What the poor young punk did not realize was this year the trick would be on him.

Amos expected few, if any, trick or treater's this year. Since the death of his wife, he had been marked by the town as an eccentric; someone to keep your kids away from. Only the small town hoodlums dared to taunt him, always teasing, always cruel. Those ones would come to his door this night. Amos sat in the rocker behind the large picture window watching the walkway. Timothy was sure to come, he always did.

A few minutes past eleven, Amos' perseverance paid off. The doorbell rang its shill buzzer repeatedly, as if a finger were stuck on the button. Amos opened the door, a broad smile on his usually somber face.

"Hey, Old Man. You'd best have some candy or something to treat me with if you know what's good for you."

"I've been waiting for you Timothy."

"Yeah, right. So what's the treat?"

"I don't have one."

"Well, you better cough up some cash then or believe me, old man, you ain't going to like my trick."

"Yes, well...maybe I can come up with something, young Timothy."

"Quit calling me that. It's just Tim. Got it?"

Amos continued to smile. "Why don't you follow me, just Tim, and I'll see what I can come up with."

Timothy stood on the porch and stared at the old man. For the first time, the kid appeared nervous. He looked over his shoulder, as if hoping that his friends were around. All he saw was an empty street. Putting his hands in his jeans pockets, he said, "Okay, show me what you got." and followed the older man inside.

Amos led him toward the stairway. He turned back and looked at the young man. The boy didn't appear to be so brave now. A look of confusion caused a deep crease to appear between the boy's brows, his dark eyes were wide and he was constantly licking his lips with his tongue as if his mouth were dry. One hand went up to push his stringy blond hair from his face.

"Where you taking me, man?" his bravado attempting to keep his fear at bay.

"Just upstairs where I keep my wallet. It is cash you want, correct?"

"Old man, you better make this worth it."

"Trust me, just Tim, this will be the most valuable treat you've ever received." Amos could see the greed in the boy's eyes. "Follow me."

Reaching the room at the end of the upstairs hall, Amos opened the door. The carefully placed candles made the room fully illuminated and by the time Timothy caught up with him, he was ready.

"What the hell?" the boy asked, catching sight of what was in the center of the room.

Before he could turn and run Amos had the chloroform soaked rag over his mouth and nose. Within moments, the young man relaxed in his arms; passed out cold.

"Well, young Timothy...excuse me, just Tim. You are in for a very special treat tonight. This will be the greatest trick I have ever done."

The older man placed the boy's body in a heavy upholstered straight back chair. Almost lovingly, he tied the young man's wrists and ankles to the arms and legs of the chair. When he was satisfied his captive was secure; he went over to his wife's cold, immobile body.

"Only a few more moments love." he said, stroking her gray, colorless face. He rose to his feet and walked to the corner where a pedestal stood centered within a circle. Walking around the circle three times clockwise, he chanted 'LUOS TSOL ESIR" redundantly. At the end of the incantation, he turned in the opposite direction and repeated the rite with a different chant.

Upon completion, he walked to the pedestal and began turning the pages of the large book placed on the stand.

Reading again the printed words, he nodded to himself and began the incantation. Over and over, he repeated the words until his voice began to crack and his throat ached. Amos felt dizzy. He could feel a presence here in this room with him. Suddenly the chair that held the bound Timothy Bryan crashed to the floor. Amos glanced at the boy, and could tell he had not yet regained consciousness. He continued with his ritual chant.

He watched as his wife's fingers began to move. Glancing at the clock on the wall, he saw it was a minute to midnight. The moment when all departed souls were free to walk the earth once more.

He chanted more fervently, knowing that his wife's spirit was now with him. His wife began moving her arms and legs until finally she was sitting in an upright position.

She shook her head. Her long blond hair flowing loosely. Taking a deep breath, she looked around the room.

"I think you can stop now, Amos. You don't want to call back more than you expect."

Amos collapsed in a heap on the floor. Tears ran from his eyes. He had done it. Laura was home now. She was alive. No longer would he be alone.

Laura stood and walked over to where Timothy lay on the floor. "Isn't that the Bryan's little boy?" A frown clouded her features. "Was he still a punk kid? I remember him."

Amos could only nod. She even had her memories. It was more than he could have ever hoped for.

"Laura, my darling Laura. You have returned to me."

For a long moment, the blond woman only stared at the man sitting on the floor in the corner. A smile broke on her lips, her eyes dancing with laughter.

"Returned to you? Not in your wildest dreams. I was leaving you when I had that damned accident. What makes you think I would stay now?"

Amos could hear the bitterness in her voice. He had forgotten that fight years before when she had walked out. All he had remembered was the devastation he felt when he learned she was dead.

"Laura, my darling, I've bought you back. Surely you won't leave me now."

"You make it sound like I owe you something. I owe you nothing. I will not be trapped in a miserable existence like before."

"I promise you Laura, it will be different. I'll make it all up to you."

"Not a chance."

With that, Laura Mallory blew her husband a kiss, turned and walked out of the room. Between his sobs, Amos heard her descend the stairs and the front door slam. He had risked everything to bring her back and now he was left with only more heartbreak, and the body of the teenager to deal with.

Hearing the sound of splintering wood, he lifted his head from his hands, hoping beyond hope that his darling had returned. What he did see was Timothy Bryan, his dark eyes now soulless white, his face contorted with rage walking toward him. It was then, he screamed.

—

DELICATE BALANCE

Jerry Thomas was frustrated. For the third week in a row the new crops were decimated. He ran the back of his rough, scarred, hand across the forehead of his weather beaten face. His shoulders slumped, making him appear much older than his forty-two years.

"Damn deer" he said as his tired blue eyes looked across the expanse of the two-acre garden plot.

He had tried everything he could think of to discourage the nocturnal browsing. From electric fences, tin pans and white sheeting hung from wires and blowing in the wind, chimes and even the dog. Nothing worked. Another old farmer suggested he urinate on the four corners of the garden. "Leave your mark" he had said. Jerry had pissed on every square inch of the garden edge. They still came.

When the garden was young and just sprouting a scarecrow had worked, but for some unknown reason the thing kept losing its head and therefore its effectiveness. So Jerry had begun sitting in the middle of the garden himself, armed with a rifle, more than willing to dispatch the pests from their hooves to his freezer. Yet the deer were smarter than he was, they just waited until exhaustion forced him to his own bed and then began another rape and pillage excursion of the garden goodies.

Jerry glanced at the headless crucified straw man in the center of the remaining plants. Maybe he should think of fashioning a head for it once again. Discouraged, he turned and walked slowly back toward the house. He knew his wife would never understand and the incessant nagging would begin once more. She counted on the garden not only for winter food, but also those blue ribbons she won yearly at the county fair for canning the vegetables. Jerry reached the stoop prepared for the worst.

"You're empty handed again." Belinda said, shaking her head, her frown showing her displeasure.

"Deer" Jerry responded, thinking no further explanation was necessary.

"Well, Jerry, you're going to have to do something about them. I should be canning green beans and tomatoes by now. I mean, good heavens Jerry, it's only 'Bambies'."

"Only deer, right." He said as he sucked in a deep breath of exasperation. He turned and went back outside not knowing what he would do, only to escape any further discussion from his wife.

Jerry entered the wooden shed thinking he would take care of the rabbits. It was time to breed a few and slaughter a few others anyway. As he made his way to the far wall, he tripped over a hoe that had fallen from its hook. Jerry found himself face down in the dirt floor of the shed. "Damn it all." He cursed loudly as he rolled over to his back. Then he saw it and smiled.

The old store mannequin was staring down at him from the rafters of the shed. It had been purchased during Belinda's sewing days. She had insisted that it was better than a dressmaker's dummy and had nagged relentlessly until he bought it for her. The long hair of its head blew gently in the breeze of the open shed door. From this angle, Jerry thought, it looked human enough. Possibly it would look human enough in the garden also. Picking himself up out of the dirt, he went for a ladder to pull the dummy down.

Three hours later, he had it done. The straw body on the crossed upright replaced with the lashed body of the mannequin. He had found old clothes of Belinda's in a truck and had dressed the dummy as outrageously as he could. Now it was time to haul it over to the garden. As he tried to position the thing to carry, he realized that he should have done the work over there to begin with. Not only was it heavy, but due to the size and shape of the thing, it was hard to maneuver. After several starts, stops and drops, he reached the center of the garden.

Looking at the bean crop next to where the scarecrow had stood only hour's earlier, he saw that his adversary had been there while he was gone. Like the outer plots of the garden, deer had already picked this harvest.

"This will stop you." He said as he looked around for signs of the deer. Lifting the mannequin into place where the straw man had once stood, he realized he was going to have to force the pole deeper into the ground to support the extra weight. He laid the dummy back on its side and headed back to the shed for the ladder and a heavy hammer. After another hour, it was in place. He stood before it and said with more hope than conviction,

"This has got to work."

"Lunch." Belinda's voice screamed across the yard to the garden.

"Well, at least she's still cooking for me." He said, aloud to the new garden guardian. He turned and walked back to the house.

That night there were neither deer, nor the next night either. For more than a week, the garden began to flourish again. Jerry picked some ripe tomatoes and almost a bushel of green beans. Belinda was happy. On the ninth morning, Jerry grabbed the basket and headed for the garden, confident that the problem had been solved.

The moment he opened the garden gate, he knew he was wrong. He watched as the last of a small herd of deer jumped the fence and disappeared into the surrounding woods. "Shit!" was all he could say as he saw not only the beans, squash, and corn devoured, on closer look he could see that almost every ripe tomato had a bite taken out of it. "Damn!"

He looked to the center of the garden. The mannequin had been toppled and its' head lay staring up to the sky several feet away. As he approached, he saw that the entire side of the dummy's head was bashed and broken. He picked up the remains and grabbing the body up, headed toward the shed.

That night he hid himself among the tall stalks of corn. His rifle crossed his lap. The full moon gave enough light to see. He waited. Hours passed, until just before dawn he heard the crunching of leaves beneath the steps of many hooves. He raised the rifle. As the first, then the second, and a third deer, jumped the fence, he waited. When he could count six, he fired. The largest deer fell with a thump to the ground. The remaining deer panicked. Fleeing here and there, trampling the garden plants, trying to make their escape. Jerry fired again. Then, again. In the end he killed three deer before the rest broke loose, back into the darkness of the woods. He sat down and waited for the light of dawn.

By mid-afternoon, he and Belinda had processed and packaged the three deer. The freezer was brimming with white paper parcels, enough to keep them in red meat for the entire winter. Wearing thick gloves, he cleaned up the shed from any remains. His eyes caught sight of the headless mannequin in the corner. Jerry picked up the largest deer head and placed it atop the pole above the dummy's body. He laughed. "Bet that would keep them from coming back." At the same time, he wondered if he dared to try it. It wasn't season; but then again, he did have the Game and Fish Department's permission to rid himself of the deer in his garden. And he had heard from an old farmer that dried deer blood would keep them out. Once more he carried the crucifix pole and its contents back to the garden.

For over a week, it worked. At least on the deer. The hot, dry weather conditions helped the garden to flourish. Now he had the problem of the stench of not only the rotting head, but also the carrion birds that came to feed off of it. He would have to think of something else. The garden was about done anyway; his spending a few more nights in it would matter little to him. Pushing the scarecrow down, he removed the head from the pole and carried it deep into the woods for disposal.

The days passed quickly, turning swiftly into autumn, with Jerry sleeping through most of the daylight hours, while sitting up in the cornfield maintaining his vigil at night. He hoped this would be his last night. There was no moon tonight, yet he had not needed a flashlight to navigate to his spot by knowing that it would only spook the deer. After twenty-two years, he knew this land as well as he knew every curve of his wife's body. The pitch-blackness of the night made it impossible for him to see if anything had jumped the fence yet. He was dogged tired. Tomorrow, he would pick anything remaining as they were calling for an early frost in two days' time. A few more hours and it would be done. All he had to do now was stay awake. His eyes were heavy, his body bone weary. Slowly, against his will, his eyes closed and he was asleep.

A flash of lightening streaked across the sky. "Where did that come from?" he wondered. There had been no rain or storms in the forecast. He heard the dried fallen leaves crackling outside the garden fence. He waited. As quiet as possible, he worked his way to the edge of the corn stalks. The garden in front of him was illuminated in an eerie blue glow. Lightening continued to flash rapidly overhead. More than twenty deer stood in his garden. They were not eating or browsing, only looking at him. Jerry felt a moments panic, then dismissed it, thinking they were just frozen to the spot by fear from his appearance in the corn.

He stood and watched in awe as the largest buck deer he had ever seen approached him. He heard it speak,

"For years we have lived a delicate balance. We eat your gardens, you eat our meat. It has been a fair trade--one always trying to outwit the other. You have broken the rules and upset that balance. We mourned when you killed the three of our kind, but we accepted it. Yet what you did with the head, that was a desecration and a shame. We have to return the balance."

Jerry looked at the deer, which had circled around him. "I've fallen asleep and this is a dream" he thought. Moments later, the large buck stepped back a few steps, lowered his head and plunged his antlers into the midsection of Jerry Thomas' body. He collapsed to the ground, pain tearing at every organ of his stomach, lungs, and abdomen. "It has to be a dream," Jerry thought as his own blood nourished the ground beneath his fallen body. And then, he thought no more.

THE WELL

Sarah Lewis leaned against her kitchen sink, closer to tears now than when the well first went out two weeks ago.

Mr. Palmer, stood opposite her against the kitchen door, ashen faced and mumbling about not being able to fix the problem.

"But I don't understand, Mr. Palmer," she said, twisting a strand of her bright auburn hair. "You told me on the phone that digging a collapsed well wasn't that big of a job. I mean, I know it's hard work, but you said you would be able to do it."

"I know, Miz Lewis, but that was before I looked at the thing. Why, it was still crumbling down, while I was in there. It's just not safe, right now, to fix it. If I was you, I'd put in a cistern, have my water hauled and just forget about that old well. Or better yet, dump this place fast and find somewhere with city water."

"That's easier said than done, Mr. Palmer," she replied. "After all, this is my home. Maybe I'll think about that cistern. But God only knows where I'll get the money."

"Well think hard about that other option I said, Missy."

"I'll call you when I decide about the cistern, Mr. Palmer."

"'Fraid I don't do that kind of work anymore. You'll have to check the yellow pages to find someone that does," she said, never meeting her eyes.

"Well, then, what do I owe you, Mr. Palmer." Sarah said.

"Never mind that. Right now, I've just got to get on to my next call. Think about what I said, would you ma'am?"

That said, the man turned and left. Sarah could swear that she heard the tires of his van throwing rocks as he pulled out of the drive. She sat down at the table and tried to think.

She supposed she should just start calling other plumbers listed in the phone book. Only in desperation would she call the man she had working in the house before, she just didn't like his whole attitude. The last time he had been here, he spent the day propositioning her and trying to touch her in places she couldn't handle.

After going after the phone book, she began calling the numbers listed for well and cistern plumbers. Each call received the same answer. Either they didn't do that kind of work anymore or they were too busy to even come check the problem out. There was only one number left to call, feeling like she had no choice left, she called the plumber she detested.

When he finally answered on the other end, he told her that it would be at least a week or maybe two before he could come out to work on the well.

"But, I'll be happy to drop some water by, if you need it bad enough to grant me a favor or two," he replied.

"Damn" was all she said, as she slammed down the phone.

"Now what?" She asked herself aloud. She just didn't know. Frustrated and angry over the whole situation, she knew she just as well go get the kids from her sister's house. She needed to fill up the water jugs again anyway. Taking her keys from the center of the table, she got up and left the house.

As she got into her truck, she let the thought of burning the house to the ground cross her mind.

***

Two days later, she had reached a decision. If she couldn't get anyone else to dig the damn well out, she would do it herself. She knew she could leave the children with her sister during the day. That way she could work and not have to worry about what they were into. She just hoped that Amy wouldn't mind her cleaning up at her house every night. Maybe if she offered to pay her water bill that would never become a problem.

Picking up the phone she dialed her sister's number to discuss her plans. Sarah knew it would take her at least a couple of weeks to get the job done, and she could afford to pay Amy a small amount to baby sit. Amy, being a single mother like herself, could always use the money.

The following morning, after she had dropped the kids off, she armed herself with a flashlight and headed for the well. Hesitantly, she peered over the stone wall, but even with the light, she could see nothing. Summoning up her courage, she climbed over the wall to the ladder and began her descent. The flashlight, now hanging from a loop on her jeans, did little to illuminate the gloom below her. Finally she reached the bottom.

Taking the final step, she found herself standing knee deep in water.

"What the hell?" She said aloud, as she cast the light around her. The water was perfectly clear, with no signs of cave in. The pump was entirely submerged in the cool liquid.

As she stood in amazement, trying to understand what was going on, a voice called out from the ladder behind her.

Swinging around, her light fell on what appeared to be a woman sitting on the rungs of the ladder.

"It took you long enough to come down here to check this out for yourself, my dear Sarah." The woman-thing said.

Sarah was still too taken aback to answer, her mind, still trying to understand what she saw. Before her was a creature, one that had a beautiful face and well developed upper body. But the feet, which were balanced on the ladder rung beneath her, were shaped like the goats Sarah had grazing in the pasture. She was blond and was wearing a long flowing dress the color of fall moss. The emerald green eyes that glared back at her made Sarah's own green eyes pale and lifeless by comparison.

"What are you?" was the only reply that came from her lips.

"What am I? What an original question. I have been asked that so many times in the past, it's becoming tiresome." The thing answered. "I suppose, if we are to get anywhere at all, I just as well try to explain. Although, in this day and time, I am sure you'll never really understand. I am a Glaistig, a water fairy of sorts, if that makes it any easier."

"But what are you doing here? In my well?" Sarah asked.

"I live here, of course. I have for ages. Do you have any idea of how old this well is anyway?" The she-creature responded.

Sarah, still in shock, dumbly shook her head no.

"They dug this well when the house was built, back in 1912. Until then, I had lived in a stream near here. Suddenly, when the water was tapped for this, I found myself here, inside this walled contraption, with no way get out. You see, my feet won't let me climb." With that she lifted her skirts to show that her lower body was indeed that of a hoofed animal.

"But how do you live?" Sarah asked, not quite believing anything she was hearing. She had, up to this moment, never regarded fairies as true beings. When she thought of fairies, she thought of Tinkerbelle or some other tiny creature from a Disney movie.

"You see, my dear, that's where you come in. Every five years, I eat. And you get to feed me."

"I get to feed you? Feed you what?" She questioned cautiously.

"A man, obviously. A strong, healthy, viral man. Preferably one that is good to look at. You know what I mean dearie. One like that farmer who used to call on you."

"Todd? How did you know about Todd?" Sarah could hear the panic rising in her voice.

"I know everything that goes on up at the big house.

One of my blessings, I suppose. Although I can't get out of this hole, my mind can. So I keep up with what is going on around me. But, enough idle chatter. I will offer you the same deal, I offered the man before you."

"And what's that?" Sarah asked, the fear sounding in her voice.

"It is very simple. You have forty-eight hours to bring me a man. Then you will have water again. Easy, right?"

"And if I don't? I mean, what if I just pack up the kids and leave?" She asked, fearful of the answer.

"Did you know, Sarah my dear, that young male minds are so susceptible? Your little boy, just turned seven two days ago, didn't he? He wouldn't sustain me for the full five years, but he might grant you a reprieve of six months or so.

Maybe by then, you would be more willing."

"You couldn't do that." She replied, hearing anger and pure fear rising in her voice now.

"I couldn't? Maybe you should talk to the former owner.

Ask him what he thinks. He tried to run too, but his boy came back to me."

Terrified now, Sarah reached out to push the creature away. Her arms hit bare steel. The creature was gone. As fast as she dared, she climbed the rungs of the ladder. As she was stepping over the top of the wall, she heard the voice call out, "Remember, Sarah, you only have forty-eight hours."

Racing back to the house, she tried to remember where she had put Mr. Connor's telephone number. She knew she had to talk to him. At the moment, she doubted her sanity.

Surely, he would tell her there was nothing in the well.

Searching through the papers of the kitchen junk drawer, she finally found Mr. Connor's phone number. Her hands were shaking so uncontrollably that she had to restart several times before she dialed the number correctly. Pacing the floor as it rang on the other end; she tried to calm herself so she would be able to talk coherently.

Then a male voice answered, "Hello."

"Mr. Connor? This is Sarah Lewis. Look, I know this is going to sound crazy, but I went down in the well this morning...."

Sarah was cut off mid-sentence by the sound of a choking groan on the other end. A moment later, the man responded, "I'll be right over."

Harvey Connor pulled in the driveway twenty minutes later. When he left, more than six hours had passed. By the time he finished talking; Sarah was feeling helpless, bewildered and filled with terror.

Still shaking, Sarah got up from the table and poured herself another cup of coffee. Sitting back down, she tried to think of what to do. Though Mr. Connor said that running was useless, she knew she had to try to get her children to safety. Taking her coffee upstairs, she packed a small duffel bag for the kids.

Once she had what they would need for a few days, she walked into her bedroom and got her bank book out of the night stand drawer. Opening it, she saw that she had almost eight hundred in savings. Picking up the duffel, she made her way back downstairs. Grabbing her car keys, she left the house.

As she started her truck, she wondered if she would be allowed to leave. According to Mr. Connor, this thing had amazing powers. If she could just get to the bank and then to the kids, maybe her plan would work. Putting the truck in gear, she backed slowly out of the drive.

After stopping at the bank, Sarah drove to Amy's house.

Parking in front on the street, she knew that her sister would think she was crazy.

"Maybe I am." She said aloud. But she knew, somehow she had to convince her to go along with her plan. Going up to the door and knocking, she waited until she heard Amy's voice say, "Come on in."

As she walked up the stairs, she heard Amy ask. "Well, how did it go?"

Entering the living room, Amy took one look at her and said, "Hell, you're not even dirty. Did you get it fixed already?"

Sarah sat down on the couch shaking her head no.

Seemingly looking at her for the first time, Amy asked, "Sarah, what's wrong?"

"Where are the kids?" Sarah replied.

"They're outside, why?"

"Just call them in. Tell them to play in the bedroom.

Then I'll tell you what's going on. But I've got to know where Tommy is. Okay?"

Once the kids were inside, Amy sat on the couch next to Sarah.

"Now, will you tell me what's going on? You look like hell. I can't remember seeing you like this since Thomas died."

Sarah opened her purse and took out the money. She began trying to explain, "Amy, you know how you have always believed in the supernatural? You know the things we can't explain. And how, you've always said that for every myth, there's reality behind it? Well, now I believe it too. I went down in that well this morning and found all the proof I need."

Amy looked at her skeptically and said, "What are you talking about?"

"In my well is this being. She calls herself a Glaistig. From what Mr. Connor, he's the man we bought the house from, told me, she is a malevolent entity that feeds on the blood of men. I know it sounds crazy, but I swear Amy, it's true. Mr. Connor lost his only child to this thing. And now, if I don't bring her a man, she's coming after Tommy."

"Sarah, are you sure you didn't hit your head down in that well?" Amy asked, "I mean this does sound just a little far-fetched."

"I know it does. I wouldn't believe any of this if I hadn't seen her with my own eyes. But even if you don't believe me, humor me, please. Here, take this," she said, pressing the money into Amy's hand, "and go visit Aunt Ida or something. I don't care what, just take the children and go." Reaching again into her purse, "Take my gas card too. Please, go, and don't let Tommy out of your sight."

"If I didn't know that this money was for taxes, I would think you were crazy. But I do know how you've had to scrimp to save this. So I've got to believe something is going on.

Okay. We'll go. I don't like leaving you here alone to face whatever is going on though."

"I'll be all right, just please, and watch over Tommy for me. I'll call Aunt Ida's when I know it's safe to come back."

Calling the kids in, she told them they were going on vacation with Aunt Amy. Kissing her small children goodbye an hour later at Amy's car, she wondered if she would ever see them again. After watching them until they were out of sight, she got back in her truck and headed downtown to the library.

She hoped they would have some information, somewhere, that could help her in dealing with this creature. Only at last resort would she call the number Amy had pressed into her hand just before leaving.

"Call him," she had said, "of all the people I know who deal with this subject, he's the one that may be able to help you.

* * *

Several hours later, Sarah heard the announcement over the loudspeaker that the library was closing in five minutes.

Except a few brief passages, she had found nothing at all to help her. Taking the books to the Xerox machine, she made copies of what little there was. Gathering up her belongings, she knew that she had to eat. Maybe then, she could think better.

As she was getting ready to leave, she saw a man come in the doors. Stopping momentarily, he looked around the large room. A few moments later, he walked up to Sarah.

"Excuse me, but are you Sarah Lewis?" The man asked, his voice strong yet somehow tender.

"Yes, but do I know you?" She asked in reply.

"No, your sister Amy does. She called me a little while ago and told me you were here. She also told me about your problem." He said.

"She did?"

"Amy also told me to tell you that they have made good time, she's more than two hundred miles away. And that Tommy is fine."

"But who are you?" Sarah asked, once again.

"Amy said she gave you my number, but she was sure you wouldn't call. My name is John Aaronson, but my friends call me Jack. Why don't we go get a cup of coffee, where we can talk?" He asked.

"I was just on my way to get something to eat, why don't you join me?" she replied.

Sarah still wasn't sure of this man, but felt as long as they stayed in public places, she would be all right.

Looking at him she could understand part of the reason her sister knew him. If she put him on a scale of one to ten in the looks department, he would come out somewhere closer to a twelve.

Normally she wasn't attracted to dark haired men, but his ebony black hair and eyes of the same color, came together to give him a very striking, mysterious look. He was taller than Sarah's own five foot nine, maybe by an inch or two, ruggedly built and looked as if he were more comfortable in the jeans he was wearing, than anything else.

Walking the two blocks to the nearest restaurant, Jack told her more about himself. He explained that he was an anthropologist who specialized in the basis of myth and fairy tales. For the moment he was teaching at the State College over on the west side of town. Another six months would find him back in the field, doing research and training selected students in his field.

"And yes," he said as they reached the Diner, "I do believe that many of the legendary creatures do exist. Such as the one in your well."

Once they were seated at a table, Sarah asked,

"Okay. You say you believe about the Glaistig. My question is, what the hell do I do now? There's no way I'm going to give her a 'sacrifice'.

"No, I didn't think so," she said, half grinning. "First off, how long do we have to your deadline?"

Sarah looked down at her watch, then said, "Well, it's ten o'clock now, so that leaves me about thirty-five hours."

"That doesn't give us much time, but more than I thought we had. Here's my suggestion. Come with me over to the university. Together, with both of us searching, I think we might be able to come up with some way to defeat this creature."

"Do you think we really have a chance?" she asked.

"The odds are probably against us, but right now, I don't have any other ideas, do you?" He replied.

"No." was the only answer she could give.

As soon as Sarah had eaten her fill, they left the restaurant. She followed him in her truck until they reached his campus office. Once inside, she was amazed at the number of books lining the walls.

Noticing her awe, he said, "Yes, we have to go through most of those. And if we find nothing there, then we'll hit the ones in the store room."

"Then I guess we best get started. Where do we begin?" she asked.

Walking across the room, he pulled several large volumes from an upper shelf. Handing them to her, he said, "Use the indexes. Look up everything on fairies, trolls, goblins and of course a Glaistig. But I doubt if we'll be that lucky."

Taking the books to a large table, Sarah began. As the hours passed, more books were perused. She was only slightly aware of the coffee cup that appeared in front of her. Even less conscious of that she was drinking it and that the mug was being refilled as it was emptied.

As daylight began to break through the open windows, she finally stood up and stretched. She was surprised that sometime in the night, they had been joined by another young man.

Walking over to Jack, she whispered, "Who is that?"

"Frank. He's one of my interns. Thought we might need him to help with the research. Not to mention the coffee."

"Does he believe what we're looking for?" she asked.

"No. I didn't even try to explain. He understands that it's his job, just to come in when I call and do whatever I need doing. I figure the less who know, the better off we are. Right?"

"You just don't want to appear crazy to your students, that's all," she said. "Did you find anything at all about this creature? I know I didn't."

"Maybe. Let's go get some breakfast and I'll tell you what I know."

"Breakfast does sound good. But I hope that 'maybe' will sound a little more positive after we've talked about it," she replied.

Over a breakfast of meatless Eggs Benedict, Jack told Sarah of his plan.

"What I'm going to suggest is going to be risky as hell.

In fact it's downright dangerous. But it is the only way I can come up with to rid you of this problem. Are you willing to listen?"

"Jack, you're the only hope I have of keeping my home.

If we can't find a way to get that creature out of my well, then I'll have nowhere to live. Lord knows, I would never sell the house to anyone knowing what's down in that well. So yes, I'm listening."

"All right then, here goes. From what I could dig up last night in the books, this Glaistig is almost indestructible. Except, when feeding time falls on the full moon. Which is tomorrow night. If we can somehow stall her till then, I think a simple well-placed bullet will destroy her." he paused.

"Jack, there's got to be another way. I mean, I know what she is, but I can't justify killing it. She's a living creature and I couldn't live with myself if we destroy her." she responded.

"Sarah, I understand your feelings, but I don't see any other way. I'll make you a promise, I'll do my best not to kill it, only wound it, so we can get it out of there. Deal?"

"No, Jack, I can't agree to that. At least not yet. First I'm going to have to try to reason with it. See if she will let me try to help her escape from the well. Maybe then, a sacrifice won't be necessary."

"In other words, you would prefer to turn her loose. To let her go out into the world to prey on victims at will. Sarah, I hate to say this, but then there would be more blood on your conscience than ever. Every time you read in the paper, or heard on the news, of another strange death, you would wonder if it was her. I would think, over time, feeling the way you do about life, that it would probably drive you mad." He countered.

"Oh God, I'm so confused." She said, "I don't know what to do. Either way, I feel I'm damned."

"Sarah, innocent people don't deserve to die. Did Mr. Connor's little boy even have a chance? And what about the others that went before and after him? Did they deserve to die?" He asked.

"All right, you've made your point. What is it I have to do?" she answered.

"In order to buy us the time we need, you're going to have to go back down there. Somehow you've got to convince her that you've got her 'her victim'. But you can't deliver till after dark."

"Okay. But not just yet, I've still got to try to get this settled in my mind. Can I do it later this afternoon?" She asked.

"I was thinking more like in the morning, about the time of you deadline. I think it will be more convincing then," she said.

"But, Jack, what about this mind-link she can do? I mean, won't she know that I'm setting a trap?" Sarah asked.

"First off, I don't think she can link with the female mind. That's why her victims have to be male. Second, just in case I'm wrong, I'm going to put you in a state of hypnosis while you're down there. That way your mind will be closed to her. Of course, if you're willing to along with this, that is."

"Then what? Suppose this works, and I get us the time we need. I don't think I'm capable of actually shooting a living creature. Even this one."

"I didn't think you would be. That's why after dark, I'll go down. If I'm right about this, your nightmare will be over."

"Jack, I can't let you do that. I mean, it's not even your problem. What if you're wrong? That creature could destroy you instead," she said, shaking her head.

"Sarah, let me explain something to you. I've spent my entire adult life studying about entities such as her. This is my one chance, to actually see one. When I come out of that well, I'll have a treasure in the anthropology circles.

This find will make everyone sit back and rethink their positions on myths. I can't pass this up, Sarah. It's too damn important."

"Okay. I guess I can't say no to my part either, huh?"

"You know, I probably would have gone down there anyway, don't you?" he said.

"I just figured that out." She replied.

"Good, I'm glad that's settled. What do you say to us going back to my place to clean up? I know I could use a shower. Plus, I really don't think you need to be going home until we've got the details of this worked out," she said.

"A shower does sound inviting. I just wish I had a change of clothes with me. But at least, I'll be clean under my dirty clothes, right?" she replied.

"Sarah Lewis, you're one hell of a lady. Just wanted you to know that." He said.

"Thank you, kind sir. Same goes for you." She said, with her first real smile since the nightmare began.

Riding with Jack, Sarah discovered that he lived in a small house, off campus. Pulling into the drive, he cautioned her not to mind the mess and to make herself at home. Inside, she found it neater than he had led her to believe. Setting her purse on the sofa, she watched as Jack went down the hall and into another room. Moments later he returned and handed her a pale-blue silk dress shirt.

"If you want, you can wear that and I'll throw your clothes in the washer for you. If not, I understand," she said, a half grin forming on his lips.

"Modesty was never one of my greater virtues," she said, "Besides, I've always loved the feel of silk."

Taking the shirt from him, Sarah felt the chemistry between them begin to build. They stood, staring at each other until Jack finally said, "Ladies first. The shower's the second door on the left."

Pulling her hand from his, Sarah replied, "Right." and walked down the hall. While in the shower, she wondered if her attraction to Jack was just because of the danger they were in. At the moment all she could think about was how much she wanted him. Wanting him to kiss her and wanting to make love to him. This was the first time she had felt this way about a man since her husband had died four years ago. If anything happened before tomorrow night, she knew she would never regret it.

Stepping out of the shower and toweling off, she slid her arms into the sleeves of the shirt. Buttoning down the front, she could still smell Jack's cologne in the collar.

Breathing it in deeply, she wished she could just cuddle up to him and that smell and forget the horror of what lay in front of them both.

Sighing, she gathered up her dirty clothes and opened the bathroom door. Walking up the hall, she saw that Jack was in the kitchen making coffee. Going through the doorway, she said, "Your turn. Where's the washing machine and I'll get these started. You got anything to put in with them?"

"The machine is out on the side porch. You can check the hamper there, I don't know what all is in there. If you want, while I'm in the shower, you can lie down and take a catnap. I'll wake you when I get out. The bedrooms down the hall and left."

"I think I'm too wired up to sleep, but maybe I'll stretch out on the sofa till you get done. Will that be all right?" she asked.

"You bet." he replied, then was gone down the hall.

Sarah wasn't sure how long she had been asleep. She only knew that it had been light and restless. She couldn't stop dreaming about that creature and what it would do to Tommy if something went wrong. Jerking awake, she found Jack sitting on the floor beside the couch.

"How long did I sleep?" she asked.

"Not long, maybe an hour. But I could tell it wasn't peaceful. Want to talk about it?" he said.

"God, Jack. It was terrible. I kept seeing this picture of that thing with Tommy. Damn, I just can't shake how real it seemed." She said.

Jack pulled himself up on the couch beside her. Putting his arms around her, and holding her close as she cried, he whispered that it was going to be all right. Finally, Sarah composed herself and pulled back to look at him.

"I'm O.K. now. Honest. Sorry about that. I didn't mean to come apart like I did." She said.

"Frankly, I'm surprised it didn't happen before now. Like I said before, you're one hell of a lady, Sarah Lewis."

Taking her face in his hands, he used a finger to wipe a lingering tear away. The next moment he kissed her softly. Within seconds, the kisses became deeper and more passionate as they clung to one another on the couch.

Finally pulling away he looked at her and said, "I want you, Sarah Lewis. Any objections?"

"None." was her only reply, as he gently picked her up and carried her toward the bedroom. Sarah was still unsure of whether it was her fear that fueled her passion, but really didn't care. As they slowly explored each other's bodies, she allowed herself to be cradled by the intimacy they were sharing.

When at last their energy was spent, Sarah molded her body next to his on the bed. Curled within the protection of his arms, she knew she had found the person she wanted to spend the rest of her life with.

"Sarah?" Jack said, taking her away from her thoughts.

"Hum?"

"I want you to know, I don't want it to end here. After tomorrow, I still want there to be a you and me.

Understand?"

"I understand. And I want it too," she said, as she lifted her head to kiss him. She knew it was crazy, but she had quickly fallen in love with this man. Then again, she thought, maybe it's not so crazy after all.

"You know, we really should get to work. I don't even know how good of a hypnosis subject you're going to make.

After all, it's obvious you have a will of steel. I think we should practice a few trial runs."

"Whatever you say, boss. But do we have to get out of bed?" she answered with a grin.

"I think we had better. Don't think we would get much accomplished in the way of work otherwise," she said, swinging his legs over the side of the bed.

Sarah followed and reached for the shirt on the floor.

"You know, I bet my clothes are ready for the dryer now," she said.

"They're already dry." he replied, "But, I like you better in the shirt."

"The shirt it is then," she said.

As they spent the afternoon working, the grim reality of what they were trying to accomplish hit Sarah with depressing force. Although Jack had found that she did, indeed, make a good hypnosis subject, she could not shake her feeling of doom for them both.

Even after Amy had called assuring her that they had reached Aunt Ida's with no difficulty, part of her still doubted whether Tommy was safe. Pictures of what Mr. Connor had told her still ran through her mind. She knew she couldn't bear it if she had to bring Tommy's small body out of the well.

During dinner, Sarah only picked at her food. She watched Jack as he ate and wished she could detach herself from the problem as he had. He had been talking, between bites, as if tomorrow was just an ordinary day. She supposed that maybe his excitement over the creature was greater than his fear.

As Jack finished his meal, he noticed Sarah's lack of appetite for the first time.

"Hey kid, I know I'm not the best cook in the world, but I'm not the worst either. You know, you need to eat. You're going to need your strength tomorrow," she said.

"I know," she replied, "but right now food is the last thing on my mind. I just can't think of anything but the danger we're in."

"Then let me get this stuff cleared away and we'll talk about it before bed. How's that?"

"Do you really think I'll be able to sleep tonight?" she asked.

"Yes, I do. As a matter of fact, I know you will. I planted the suggestion while we were working this afternoon. Hope you don't mind too much, but you are going to need to keep your wits about you in the morning."

"Do you know this has to be the longest two days, I've ever lived through? I just wish tomorrow were behind us, so I could begin to forget." She said.

"Twenty-four more hours and it will be." Jack said as he finished loading the dishwasher. "Then we'll talk about where we're going. But right now, let's go to bed."

"O.K," she said, as she got up to follow him down the hallway.

Jack hypnotic suggestion worked, Sarah discovered as she cuddled close to his body. As soon as they had settled into position, she found she could no longer keep her eyes open and fell into a deep, dreamless sleep.

As sunlight began to stream through the windows of the bedroom, Sarah slowly came awake. She felt rested and alert, but at the same time frightened and anxious about what the day would bring. Looking over at Jack, she was surprised to see that he was still asleep. Carefully she pushed back the covers, got up and headed for the kitchen to make coffee.

As the coffee finished brewing, Jack groggily walked into the kitchen. As he sat down at the table, Sarah poured both of them a cup.

"Thanks," she said.

"You're welcome," she replied. "Do you want me to fix us some breakfast or do you want to go out."

"Let's go out. This morning is going to be hard enough, without having to worry about cooking."

Just as they finished dressing and were heading out the door, the telephone rang. Jack turned to answer it. Picking up the receiver and listening for a few moments, he said only, "Yes, I'll have to tell her. It does present a problem."

Turning back to Sarah, he took her hand and led her over to the couch. Placing his arms on her shoulders, he lowered her into a sitting position.

"Sarah that was Amy. Now listen carefully. Her son took her car sometime in the night. He and Tommy are both gone."

"Oh my God." Sarah said, feeling the fear wash over her.

"Calm down. Panic isn't going to help us here. Look, we can still get down there and bargain with her before they have time to get home. Think you can hold together that long?"

Sarah eyes were brimmed with tears as she looked at him and answered, "I guess I have too, don't I?"

"You can do it. Now, come on, let's get this over with. First, we eat. I want you to calm down some before you face that thing. The boys are still far away. Amy said she didn't get to bed till after three. They didn't leave before then. It's at least an eleven hour trip. So we've got time. O.K?"

"Yea, O.K." She said, not feeling anything near reassurance.

Two and a half hours later, they were back at her truck.

"You know what you're supposed to do, right?" he asked.

"Remember, I won't be very far away. If you don't meet me at the convenience store within forty-five minutes after your call, I'm coming after you."

"Jack, I'm scared." She said. "What if she refuses?"

"Just know that Tommy can't make it back before we have a deal with this thing. Amy has already called the police and there's an A.P.B. out on the car and the kids. With any luck, the police will pick them up long before they can reach anywhere near here. Even if they don't, the Glaistig wants a grown man, not young boys. Remember, she even told you that. I think if you can get her to agree with your deal, she will leave the boys alone. So don't panic. Everything will work out all right. This creature can't hurt you."

Taking her in his arms, he kissed her goodbye. As she got into her truck and started it, she looked in the rear view mirror at him.

"I hope you're right, Jack. I hope you're right." She said.

Pulling into her drive, Sarah had to fight with herself to keep herself from looking toward the well-house.

Jack had told her to go straight to the house and call him before doing anything. Parking the truck, she got out and went into the house. Inside, she was assaulted by the smell of burnt coffee. Walking over to the coffee maker she turned the button to off. Looking at the pot, she realized it would have to be replaced. Shaking her head, she picked up the telephone receiver and dialed the number Jack had given her.

The phone at the other end was answered on the first ring.

"Sarah?" Jack's voice came through the line.

"It's me. I'm home. Now what?" Sarah asked.

"Now I want you to take a deep breath and begin to relax. You know deep in yourself it is going to work out just fine. Keep breathing deeply, and keep that calm until your part is over. You're going to be fine. Just do what you have to do. Then call me when you're back at the house." Jack said.

"O.K. I'll call back just as soon as I can." Sarah said, feeling surprisingly calm, as she hung up the phone.

Reaching for the flashlight on the counter, she picked it up and checked the batteries. Satisfied it was working properly, she walked back across the kitchen and out the back door. As she walked the short distance to the well, she tried to remember everything Jack had told her. "Just keep breathing deeply." her mind told her over and over.

Moments later, she arrived at the well. Walking to the edge of the well itself, she took another deep breath before turning on the flashlight and climbing over the top to the first rung of the ladder. With each step she took down, she was filled with more confidence. By the time she reached the bottom, she knew they were going to win.

Taking the light from her belt loop, she flashed it around the dark interior of the well. As the light reached the pressure tank, she once again heard the voice behind her.

"Where have you been, Sarah? I was beginning to think you had forgotten about me." The Glaistig said.

"How could I forget?" Sarah replied.

"So where is my man, dearie?" The she-creature said.

"That's why I'm down here. I found someone. Everything you said you wanted. There's only one problem, I can't get him here until tonight."

"Why tonight?" it asked, "Why not now?"

"Because he had to go to work today. Look I already had to spend the night with him last night. He thinks he's coming for more of the same tonight. When he gets here, he promised to come down and see if he can find the problem.

After that he's all yours. That's the best I can do." Sarah said.

"And do you promise that he is worth the wait, Sarah dear?"

"Yes, I swear it. In fact, if circumstances were different, I could probably fall in love with him myself."

Sarah replied.

"Then you have done well. I will give you till midnight to send him to me. That way you, yourself, will have one more chance with him to see what might have been. And if you somehow forget your deadline, I'm sure you realize by now, that the children are on their way here. Midnight, Sarah, or you can say goodbye to both your son and your nephew. Now go, I am tired of talking with you."

Once again Sarah was alone in the well. Sarah made her way back to the ladder and began to climb. Almost running back to the house, she couldn't believe that it had gone so well. Jack was right. The Glaistig could not read her mind. Nor could it harm her. In the house, she grabbed the phone and dialed.

When Jack answered on the other end, she said only, "I'm on my way."

Going back out to the truck, she knew she had to keep her excitement under control until she left her property.

Doing her best not to drive too fast, she made her way to the convenience store where she knew Jack would be waiting.

At the store, Sarah pulled her truck into an empty space by Jack's small car. Opening the door, and jumping out, she looked around for Jack. Seconds later he appeared from inside the store.

Running up to him, she put her arms around his neck and said, "She agreed to it, Jack. We have until midnight."

"See, I told you she would agree. O.K. Come on, we've got a lot to do this afternoon. We need to drop your truck off somewhere close, so you can pick it up later," she said, handing her a cup of coffee from the bag he was carrying.

"There's the department store, down the street," she replied. "But what about Tommy and Neal. What if they get back before I do?"

"Sarah, there's no way they will get here before four or five this afternoon. By then you will be home, waiting for me. I promise, nothing's going to happen to the boys." He answered.

"All right, so what is it we have to do?" She asked.

"Well, first I've got to make a stop by the house of a colleague of mine. Then back by the university, to pick up the items we'll need to pull the Glaistig's body from the well. That is, if there's a body to pull. For all I know, it may just disappear after it's destroyed. After that, we can go home and relax until dark." He said.

"Oh," she replied, "Whose house are we going to? I thought you said you wanted as few people in on this as possible."

"I still do. But he has something I need. I'm not going to tell him why I need it, but he owes me a few favors so it won't be any problem getting it." Jack said.

"You've got me curious now. What is it we are going after?" She asked.

Jack flashed her sort of half grin and answered, "I know this is going to sound pretty stupid, but I'm going to get a few silver bullets from him. I don't know if there's anything to the myth of silver killing evil things, but I figure why take the chance."

"For some reason, that makes perfect sense to me." She replied.

After parking her truck in a nearby department store parking lot, Sarah rode with Jack to Ansil Stoner's home.

Sarah was surprised when they were greeted at the door by a frail elderly man who appeared to be at least ninety. Jack introduced her to him as his new assistant on a soon to be announced major project. The old man simply nodded his head, and motioned for them to enter.

Once inside and in his study, Jack asked for the bullets. Without batting an eye, the old man walked to a cabinet in the corner and withdrew a small box. Counting out six of the small cartridges, he turned and handed them to Jack.

"I suppose you need something to shoot them with?" He asked.

"Yes, Ansil, I do." Jack replied. "Tomorrow I'll have you come to the office and I will explain everything."

"From all appearances, my friend, I will pray that you will be in your office then." The old man said as he pressed a small revolver into Jack's hand.

"Thanks, Ansil. We probably do need your prayers. We really need to go now, but I will call you tomorrow."

Back in the car, Sarah asked, "Why would someone like him have silver bullets around?"

"It's simple," Jack replied, "he truly believes that creatures such as vampires and werewolves do exist. He would have no trouble accepting that thing down in your well.

That's one of the reasons, I'm going to call him in on this thing tomorrow. His name is highly respected."

"But what if you don't have a body? Who is going to believe any of this happened?" She asked.

"Ansil will." He replied.

They rode the rest of the way to the campus in silence.

Both of them lost in their own thoughts. Once in his office, Sarah watched as Jack gathered up the objects he felt he would need. The rope and black plastic she understood, but when he returned from the storeroom with iron manacles, she had to ask, "What are those for?"

"Just in case she doesn't die. At least, we can subdue her."

After he put everything into a large canvas pack, he slung the strap over his shoulder and said,

"I guess that does it. I think I've got everything."

Sarah wasn't sure who he reminded her more of: Humphrey Bogart or Indiana Jones, as they headed back to his car.

As they headed back to her truck, Jack tried to assure her that everything was going to work out. He promised to be at the house as soon as it got dark.

"I really don't want to leave you like this, but I don't see we have a choice. Just go home and remain calm. Keep watch on the well from a window. If you see the boys, and I don't think you will, go out and drag them into the house. Remind that thing of your deal, if you have to."

"God, Jack, I wish you were coming with me. I'll probably go crazy sitting in that house alone." She said.

"Well, call Amy. Ask her if she's had any word yet. Call some of your other friends, anything to keep your mind busy until I get there. All right?" He asked.

Sarah just nodded her head in agreement. She still wasn't convinced.

"A few more hours and this will be over. One way or another," she said, putting his arms around her.

"Jack, that sounds like you have doubts." She said.

"It never pays to get overconfident, love," she said, "I don't really have doubts, but there are always other possibilities."

Driving away from the city, to her house, Sarah thought she had never seen so much traffic. She couldn't remember the last time it had taken her more than thirty minutes to commute from the department store to her house. For a fleeting moment, she began to wonder if somehow the Glaistig wasn't causing this too. But then, she dismissed the thought from her mind. After all, cars were machines and half the vehicles in front of her had women drivers. She knew the creature couldn't be controlling them.

Finally, she pulled into her own driveway. Looking over to the well, she muttered, "Remember, you promised."

Pulling up in front of the house, she turned the truck off and got out. Resisting the urge to go back to the well, she went inside. Looking up at the kitchen clock, she saw that it was already after four. Four more hours and it would be dark, then Jack would be here.

She still didn't know how she was going to survive the next few hours. Her mind was reeling from fear, both for the boys and for herself and Jack. As much as she tried to believe, close to the surface was the fear that she would lose them all.

She decided to go upstairs to her bedroom, where she could watch the well while she called Amy. Once there, she picked up the phone and called Aunt Ida's house. After talking to Aunt Ida for a few minutes, Sarah waited for Amy to come on the line.

"I really let you down this time, didn't I?" Amy's voice said when she picked it up.

"It wasn't your fault." Sarah replied, "Have you heard anything from the police yet?"

"No, they're still looking. I had to lie and say that Tommy was on special medication to even get them to start searching," she replied.

"Aunt Ida doesn't know what's going on, does she?" Sarah asked.

"No, I just told her that Neil and I had been having typical mother and teenage son problems and that he ran away. She thinks that he just took Tommy along for the ride."

"Well, I just hope to God that that's all it turns out to be. Jack should be here in a few hours. I keep praying that now that this thing has made a deal, she will stick to it."

"I'm sure Jack will know how to fix the problem when he gets there. After all, that is his field." Amy said.

Sarah was surprised that Amy understood that they had to watch what they said over the phone. She was sure that the creature, while it might not be able to read female minds, could hear every word they were saying. Chit-chatting a while longer, Sarah finally rung off, telling her to call if she heard anything.

The thought hit her that maybe she should call the police at this end. Just tell them that the boys were out joy-riding. She was sure that her small town police department would be able to keep a better look out for the boys than the Highway Patrol. Picking up the phone, she dialed their number. Once they had the details they needed, the man on the other end assured her, "Don't worry, Mrs. Lewis. If one of our guys sees them, we'll bring them home."

Sarah said her thanks and then hung up, hoping she had done the right thing.

Sarah looked out the window and saw the sun was going down. Dusk was settling and she knew Jack should be here anytime. Going back down to the kitchen, she went through the cabinets until she found her old percolator. Once she had the coffee on, she went back into the front room to wait.

Forty-five minutes later, Jack pulled into the driveway. Going out to meet him, she wondered if this was the last bit of time she would be able to spend with him.

"Any word from the boys?" he asked, as he got out of his car.

"No," she replied, shaking her head.

"Well, I'm sure they will be home soon. All we have to do now is wait." He said.

Back in the house, they took up their position on the living room sofa. Sarah knew that they had to make this look good. She was aware, suddenly, that they were being watched. Now she understood why she had that feeling, so many times in the past. Curling into Jack's arms, she tried to show enthusiasm for the performance they were putting on. As Jack began unbuttoning her blouse, they heard a car pull in the drive.

Jumping up and running to the window, Sarah knew that it was Amy's car. Turning to Jack, she said, "The boys are here."

"Calm down. We'll go out and get them. Once we have them in the house, then we'll go back down to the well. It's time to get this over with." He said.

Almost running out the front door, she started screaming at the boys. They kept walking toward the well as if they had not heard. Catching up with them, she grabbed them both by the arm, and began trying to drag them toward the house. She looked around for Jack, but realized he must have gone back into the house.

When he reemerged, he was carrying his backpack. Jogging over to where she was, he took Neil's arm from her and tried to pull him in the opposite direction of where the boy wanted to go. A few moments later, he looked over at Sarah and said, "It's no use. They are stronger than we are. We're going to have to take them with us."

Closing the short distance left to the well, Sarah felt they were on a death walk. Once they reached the side, the boy's tried once again to pull away. Jack pushed Neil's wrist into Sarah's hand.

"Try to hold them until I'm in." He said, then swung his legs over the stone wall.

Once he had climbed over, the boys became passive, no longer resisting her grip. When Sarah felt it was safe, she let go of them and grabbed the Halogen light from the backpack. Trying to balance on the side she directed the beam into the well. She turned and looked at the boys, now sitting on the ground. They seemed dazed and confused, but she couldn't deal with them right now. Turning her attention back to the well, she watched as Jack took the final step at the bottom. Almost immediately the Glaistig appeared before him. As much as she wanted to turn away, she knew she had to watch and listen.

"Sarah has done well." the she-creature said to Jack.

"What the hell?" Jack said. Sarah could hear what sounded like fear in his voice.

"Did you know, that Sarah said she was falling in love with you? Isn't that a shame? Because she knows she will never see you again after tonight." The thing said, throwing her head back in hearty laughter.

"What do you mean, she won't see me again?" Jack asked.

"She gave you to me, my darling," she said.

Jack began backing up to the far side of the well as the Glaistig opened her arms and said,

"Come to me, Jack. Am I not pretty?"

Sarah watched from above as the creatures hands turned from human looking to oversized claws. The nails began to grow until they were sharp looking points. She watched as the creature walked toward Jack and put her arms around him. She saw the claw shaped nails sink into his back.

"What is that, Mom?" Tommy asked.

Sarah turned and saw that both boys were now standing and peering over the side at the thing below.

"I'll explain later." She said, then turned back to the well.

Sarah held her breath, waiting for Jack to do what he had come for. Time stopped as she watched Jack become limp in the entity's embrace. Finally, she heard the gun explode and saw the creature fall back into the mud below them.

Sarah looked down at Jack and said a thank you prayer that it was over. Jack was slumped against the wall, yet he was still alive and that's all that mattered to Sarah.

"Jack? Are you all right?" She called down, hearing her voice echo off the walls.

"Yeah. A little weak, but I'm O.K. Give me a minute and I'll be up."

"Is it safe to come down?" She asked.

"Yea, I think it's safe now. Bring the back pack with you." He answered.

Sarah grabbed the pack at her feet and swung her legs over the side. Looking over at the boys, she ordered them to stay where they were. At the bottom, she stayed along the sides of the well until she reached Jack. She reached out to hold him, and as he took her in his arms, she could see the wounds the creature had inflicted on his back.

"Those need attention, Jack." She said.

"I know. But first I want to get finished here." He replied taking the pack from her. He handed her the gun and continued, "I'm going to put the manacles on it now. If it moves, shoot it."

Jack walked over and lifted the Glaistig's arms. Closing the cuffs around both wrists, they saw that her hands had returned to normal. Attaching the second set around the cloven feet, Sarah was surprised when the creature turned its head toward her and said,

"You've played the game well, my dear Sarah. Thank you, for now, I'm finally free."

I WAIT

Today I disappeared I had been sitting beside a roaring fire contemplating the phrase "Do unto others . . ."

What happened next I do not know.

I must have dozed.

I awoke here.

Where is here? I do not know. I see nothing, as the room I am in has no windows. I cannot make out a door. The room is bare – four walls, a floor, a ceiling – nothing more.

I cannot hear a sound. Am I deaf? The silence is thunderous in its oppression.

My nose picks up no scents. It is as if everything here is sterile. I look down at my body and it is naked. My fingers touch, but all is smooth and flat, even the sensory perception of feel is denied to me. Only my feet feel the solid hardness of the floor.

An illusion.

I should panic, yet I do not. I feel safe and secure in this place, all the while knowing deep inside I am not.

I wait.

Will someone explain? Will I be fed? Am I dead? All questions I should want answers for. Have I been drugged? Is that why I do not care if the questions are answered or not?

I wait.

Maybe eternity is not that long.

I calm.

I turn. I kick. I feel a barrier against my feet. And yet, it is not solid; as the wall I kick gives way to my pressure.

Where am I?

My memories are fleeting. They are leaving me. Suddenly, I am a presence with no past.

No today.

No tomorrow.

The space is enveloping me. I feel crowded. How do I escape? Where am I?

Pressure.

I feel pressure bearing down on me. Where is it coming from?

Pushed.

I feel pushed. To go where? Why?

I am in a narrow passage way. I feel crowded. The pressure continues.

I smell air. Fresh air. Where is it coming from?

Pain.

I feel pain. Then all is forgotten. I remember nothing.

I am a newborn babe.

My eyes are open. I hear myself cry. I am held aloft. I hear the scream, "It's a boy."

What is a boy? I do not know.

Something rough encloses my body. It wraps around me, yet is not as comfortable as the place I was.

Arms from a stranger reach for me. I am nuzzled. I can smell the milk.

I am hungry.

Wait.

I feel pain again. Something in this small body is not right. Hands grab me from the stranger. I cannot breath. I am screaming. The light is fading. I feel blackness.

It is dark.

Where am I?

I wait.

About the author:

Kat Yares has been writing fiction her entire adult life. She is an author, screenwriter, indie movie maker and amateur photographer. Her short fiction has appeared in numerous print publications and online. She was first accepted into the Horror Writers Association in 2001 and remains a member today.

Her fiction is primarily in the horror/thriller genres. Unlike many, she writes horror not to gross out or startle her readers, but to make them think. Most of her stories are mind games and deal with mans (or woman's) inhumanity to man (or woman).

Her novella, Vengeance Is Mine, while horror, still strikes a chord for many readers as they can see correlations between the story and what is happening in today's political climate.

Her two novels, Beneath the Tor and The XIII, are both fantasy and thriller and as several readers have written to her, are bound to send her to Hades after she passes. Visit her blog (www.katyares.com) to find out more about her and the various Internet retail outlets where her books can be found.